HORROR ON THE RANGE

A UNDERTAKER BOOKS ANTHOLOGY

CONTENTS

INTRODUCTION

Have you ever seen something take on a life of its own?

When we were kicking around ideas for anthology themes, one of the ones that came up was Western Horror. I thought it would be great, do a couple stories featuring our resident western authors (myself and C.M. Saunders), get a few other authors to round out the lineup, and put a spotlight on western horror for a few moments.

Two hundred plus submissions later, I realized that western horror has a place in a lot of people's hearts.

Narrowing two hundred submissions down to eleven was not an easy task. We originally planned to take eight, plus mine and C.M.'s. I had to beg Cyan to let me take more so the decisions were easier.

But we got there.

And the results are fantastic.

Chloe York went deeper into the gore than I thought she could in "The Gut Wagoner." Scotty Milder puts a unique twist on vampire tales in "Desmodus." Michael Picco explores a Navajo legend in "All Fours." And Jenny Taylor brings female rage in "The Rattler's Bride."

Those are just four of the fantastic stories, and the others are just as good.

INTRODUCTION

So get ready to go west, and dive into *Horror on the Range*!

D.L. Winchester
Newport, TN
November 22, 2025

H
O
R

BOB
ON THE
RANGE

THE GUT WAGONER

CHLOE YORK

ABILENE ALWAYS WAITS til nightfall to sort the guts. Heaped in barrels tall as her—and she ain't a small woman—the refuse awaits her eager hands with matching need. Sleeves shoved to her elbows, she delves into bristly fur clinging to oil-slick skin pinker than sunrise, the crest of bones scraped half-clean by the butcher's blade, and her prize, her favorite sensation: the squelching press of cool entrails slithering along her skin.

"God almighty," she murmurs, granting herself a shut-eyed, ecstatic moment in the silky nest she's uncovered. Then all too quick, it's back to the necessary dividing of the offal for production. The skins for the leather tanners. Bones for tools, buttons, and fasteners. And the guts—the velvety, luscious *guts*—those belong to Abilene.

She could pull more coin selling them off as fertilizer or hell, they'd make a decent enough meal for less fortunate types. The type Abilene vowed she'd never be again. Those days died with her lily liver, clammy-handed husband.

Honest work. Grit. A strong stomach. The use of Clint's britches, boots, wide-brimmed hat and most importantly, his name. Lacking sturdiness of frame, she wasn't sure she could pull off the illusion. But by God, when she hitched their old mule to the wagon and rode into town with her practiced gravelly rasp, shorn hair, and Clint's identifying papers, nobody gave her a second glance.

Another advantage of salvaging butchery castoffs. Ordinary people don't wanna look too close. Women around these parts have jobs, sure. But not on the gut wagon. Course, she's got more than one reason to hide. Clint made sure of that.

The flickering lantern spreads her shadow across the splintered barn wall as she tugs through barrel after barrel and creates three piles.

Skins.

Bones.

And *hers.*

Her chest buzzes under bosoms flattened by a long length of cotton as she watches the last pile—her share of the spoils—grow and grow. Lavender tubes oozing viscous juices. Ropes of tangled veiny intestines. Scarlet, glistening organs like fist-sized rubies. Her jewels. Unceremoniously, she flings them onto a waxy canvas tarp spread on the dusty, hay-flecked ground. The wet *thwack* when they hit brings an expectant shiver to her limbs.

Like the wagon's floor—its slatted wood smooched with red stains—she can never wash out the cloying stench of raw meat from her barn. She'd do this outside—it's an hour's ride to the closest neighbor—but this ain't for the sky and stars to see. Those celestial bodies got nothing on Abilene's earthly delights.

Once the sellable bits are sorted and sealed in their barrels, she climbs from the wagon and assesses her gleaming hoard. Smaller than yesterday's, but progress is progress. Undressing deliberately slow, the way she used to do for Clint in the rare good days, she unwraps her binder with a relieved sigh and carefully lays her clothes aside.

Standing before the tarp in nothing but her bloomers, she drags herself down and folds herself into the offal like she's climbing into a soft bed. Her groan is girlish and foreign to her ears after so much time keeping her voice gruff and words brief. A noise so uniquely *her* that it drags a pained whimper from her chest. She slides through the guts, a hundred satiny caresses taking permanent residence in her very skin.

We got you, they tell her. *You ain't alone.*

"God almighty," she says again, pulling her knees up like a babe in its mother's arms. Or a lover's.

She closes her eyes—lashes catching on a sticky pink esophagus— and whooshes out a long, slow exhale. She goes still, sleep dragging her under its liquid wings. Just before she loses consciousness, she feels the guts tremble around her for a moment, then the wet shift of something stroking her calf.

She leaps to her feet, raining globs of meat that tumble from her bare skin as she seeks whatever's in the pile with her. A rattler? A field mouse? Grabbing a shovel perched in the corner, she swipes through the guts, hoping to spook the varmint out of hiding. These guts are hers. *Hers.* She will not have them desecrated.

But her search turns up nothing. Probably just imagining things in that halfway world between awake and asleep. Shoving a hand through her short hair, she gathers up the tarp with more than a little sorrow and hefts it to the closed barn door where she drops it with a squelch.

Then she pads to the old feeding trough she repurposed as a washtub, already filled with lukewarm well water. She bathes, scrubbing until all trace of her ritual is gone. After she dresses, she creaks open the barn doors and carries the tarp past the gate where her mule Sunny snorts at her.

"You lookin' at?" she says, pausing to stroke his velvet snout. The animal tickles her palm with his big teeth as she allows herself a smile.

About an acre from her single-room cabin, outhouse, and barn is a shallow gulch. The meaty odor from inside is overwhelming, even to her nostrils. Yet no buzzards ever descend on this valley, never so much as circle the growing heap of offal below. Nothing goes to rot there. The organs and viscera are as fresh as the moment she dropped them in.

It's a phenomenon she'd be hard-pressed to explain. Soon as she noticed it, she set aside some guts in the barn to see if they'd do the same. But while those pieces eventually decayed, the ones in the ravine kept their color and vitality and remained undisturbed. One of these days, Abilene reckons she'll fill the entire valley with guts. Oh, to swim in such a lake as that...

At the cliff's edge, she unfurls the tarp and watches her treasures splat atop the others down below. No coyotes or scavengers have touched this meat. Not even greedy flies. Like they know these guts are hers and hers alone.

Stifling a yawn, Abilene turns and walks back home.

Sunny's dragging his feet today. Abilene can't say she blames the poor beast. Another scorcher of an afternoon. The wagon rocks and rumbles beneath her, gloved hands clasping Sunny's reins as she resists the urge to speed him up.

She sold her skin-and-bone barrels this morning and had them replaced with empty ones. Once she hits the butchery and slaughterhouse, she'll have them full again. More money and best of all, more slithering guts. She's still thinking about how the pile seemed to move on its own last night. Had to be a critter. A rat or a snake. That, or she imagined it.

A bead of sweat rolls down her neck as she adjusts Clint's old hat to keep the sun out of her eyes. Then she pulls the wagon to a sudden grinding halt at what she sees outside Hank the butcher's shop. A wiry man with leathery skin hefting a crate overflowing with steaming scarlet entrails toward his own wagon.

"Hey!" she calls, nearly forgetting to adopt her gravelly tenor. "You, sir!"

His crinkled eyes find hers over the mound of guts he's straining to carry.

"Grisly stuff, ain't it?" he greets. His grin reminds her of dirty stones, gappy and yellowed. With a grunt, he shoves the crate with the guts—*her* guts—onto his wagon. Freshly varnished wood and balanced wheels pulled by a proud gray stallion. Makes her wagon look like decrepit old junk by comparison.

She takes a long beat to compose herself before screwing up her face in what she hopes is an intimidating snarl.

"Hank know yer takin' that?" she asks, climbing from her seat to hitch Sunny to a post while a man and woman strolling arm in arm pass them by with unconcealed disgust at the "grisly stuff" in his crate. Abilene inhales a sharp breath when she spies a swarm of fat black flies descending on the guts. Defiling them. The thieving bastard didn't even cover them.

The stranger's taller up close, but he's still only got an inch on her.

He holds up his hands, calloused cracks filled with dirt. The thought of those hands on her guts floods her ribcage with angry heat.

"The butcher? Course he knows. He's the one gave em to me."

Abilene's brows knit together hard enough to hurt.

"Listen, sir. I've been runnin' the gut wagon goin' on two years now," she says. "So I don't know what misapprehensions yer operating under, but those belong to me. You best be finding other work. I was here first, you understand. Nothin' personal."

The stranger—that above snakes *thief*—gives her a long, slow blink. He lifts one shoulder. Drops it. The motion causes his vest to slide open, revealing a silver pistol holstered to his hip. She stands her ground, undeterred.

"Ways I see it, a little friendly competition never hurt nobody," he says, leaning back on his polished boots. Fine hat, fine clothes, but on him, it looks like someone put a diamond necklace on a mud-slathered hog. "Say, what's yer name? You look an awful lot like someone I knew a ways back."

"Clint Jones," she blurts before the earth crashes open beneath her with the merciless certainty that this man is no stranger. She knows him. Clint's old drinking buddy. The one who used to leer at her over the men's card games while she cooked for them. Had better teeth back then, but his clothes were always threadbare and certainly his wagon wasn't near as fine as this one.

Paul Clay.

It's him. She's never been more certain of anything. And if she knows him, then he sure as hell knows her.

He cocks his head like a coyote, his even-keeled expression betraying nothing. She just gave him her dead husband's name, the one she stole after the poison did its job. What a damn fool she was to think she could outrun the past. Outrun what she did to Clint after what he did to both of them. She could run, she thinks. Turn tail and start over somewhere else. Every town has butcheries. Every town needs a gut wagon.

But her valley. Her magical ravine that the buzzards and flies steer clear of. Those precious entrails suspended in time like a slumbering princess in a fairy book. She can't leave them.

"Well, Mr. Jones," Paul Clay says. "I don't see why we can't reach some sorta understanding. How's about you take the bones and I'll handle the skins and…"

Abilene has forgotten how to breathe. Paul Clay, against all odds, has no idea who she is. Unless he's pretending. If so, he's a damn good liar.

"What'd you say?" Abilene cuts in, loosening some phlegm from her throat.

Paul Clay's horse gives a little whinny, its tail swishing the growing tangle of flies off its haunches. Maggot eggs will have settled into that open container of meat by now. Vomit roils in her stomach. All those perfect, slimy, glistening jewels *ruined*.

"Divide and conquer, Mr. Jones," Paul Clay says, arms raised like a showman. "Half and half. I'll take the skins—"

"The skins are worth most," Abilene says, recovering her wits and her outrage. "And there ain't gonna be any dividing. You can haul off what you got from Hank today, but this is my territory. Now be off with you before I'm late to the slaughterhouse. And for God's sake, cover that crate. Buzzards'll get you if yer not careful."

"Buzzards'll get me, huh?" he says slowly, his jovial facade fading as he curves his thumbs through his belt loops and sways on his feet. "That's funny."

Without another word, he unhitches his horse and climbs into his seat. Abilene's shoulders unclench, her breaths blessedly steadier. Paul Clay's leaving. She lost whatever's in that crate today—Hank's gonna get an earful about that—but at least her livelihood and more importantly, her identity, are safe.

Then Paul Clay twists back, lighting up a pipe. Acrid clouds billow around his wizened fox face when he shoots her a wink.

"Shame we couldn't be friends, *Mister* Jones. Friends are real hard to come by nowadays and even easier to lose. Especially when the chips are down, so to speak." He gives her another long, appraising look, rheumy eyes lingering too long on her flattened chest. "You a gambler, Jones?"

Abilene crosses her broad arms, training her terror-stricken face into the picture of masculine nonchalance.

"Can't say I am."

Paul Clay puffs out a smoke ring.

"I had a friend once. Real taste for poker. You ever played?"

She shakes her head.

"Funny thing. For a man so smitten with the game, you'd think he'd at least be half good at it. But I'll tell you, my friend was pretty nigh hopeless. What you might call an easy mark." Paul Clay takes another drag from his pipe, locking eyes with hers. "If I told you how much that yella-bellied sumbitch owed me, whew!" A humorless laugh. "And when I came to collect it, you know what I found?"

Abilene presses her hands into her armpits to stop their shaking. When he realizes she has no intention of answering, he supplies, "A damn fire! Whole place and everything in it, just..." He makes a sharp whooshing sound. "Gone." A noiseless chuckle. "You ask me, luckiest thing to happen to that man besides that wife of his. Real hellcat, that one. I always wonder what became of her. They never did turn up her body after that fire. Makes a fella wonder, don't it?"

Her nostrils flare, spine so rigid she thinks it might snap.

He knows.

He knows, he knows, he—

"Well," she says. "Like I said, you best be going before that meat spoils."

"Of course, Jonesy. Of course." Still sucking his pipe, he flicks his horse's reins and ambles down the road. Over his shoulder, he calls back, "Apologies for horning in on your *offal* business. Hah! Get it? Offal, awful..."

But Abilene is already back in her wagon ready to snap Sunny to action the second Paul Clay's outta sight, which doesn't take all that long. His wagon veers left by the general store and he's gone. But, she thinks grimly, it ain't over.

Abilene's too worked up over what happened in town to enjoy her ritual tonight. She labors over her barrels with precious little pleasure, piling jawbones and femurs into their respective places and hairy pelts and flesh into theirs.

She still flings the lovely guts to their waxy canvas sheet on the barn floor. Still plans to haul them to the valley afterward. It brings an ache to her heart knowing that bastard Paul Clay's taken half of the magic gulch's offering, but God knows he coulda taken a lot more.

She wonders why he walked away from her today. He could've blackmailed her. Taken her gut wagon duties away. Extorted her earnings or worst of all, taken from her what Clint offered in a fit of cowardly desperation. Why didn't he?

Maybe he figures Clint's untimely death was enough to settle his poker debt. Maybe he's grateful she saved him the trouble of killing Clint himself. Maybe he's even a little scared of her because of it.

But Abilene's a smart woman. She knows Paul Clay's kind. He's letting her squirm before he moves in for the kill. It's just a question of when. To be sure, she's got her loaded pistol tucked in the back of her pants. Ready as she'll ever be. She ain't running yet.

When she's done with the sorting, she scrubs her forearms clean at the trough and bundles up her guts for the gulch. Oil lantern in one hand and the heaving sack slung over her shoulder, she opens the barn door and is immediately met with the unmistakable *click* of a gun cocking.

Click click click.

No. *Guns* cocking.

Her throat floods with ice as she scans the silhouetted figures waiting between her and the valley. Without looking away, she sets down the lantern and the tarp, its edges unfurling to reveal the organs and viscera it's cradling. Through her terror, she notices a brief flurry of movement coming from inside the tarp. That same effortful slithering she felt on her skin last night. But she ain't got time to look closer. Not with those four barrels trained on her.

Damp hands raised in surrender, she finds Paul Clay's cracked tombstone smile and sets her own mouth in a grim line.

"Coin's in the house," she says, maintaining her deep voice out of habit, but she knows it won't do a damn bit of good. Paul Clay knows who she really is. That's why he's here. "In a pouch in the old steamer trunk by the stove. And the slaughterhouse haul in the barn. All yours."

Paul Clay laughs.

"That'd be a start, missus. But that husband o'yers promised somethin' a little more than money. Or did he neglect to tell you?"

Abilene's nostrils flare. No more pretense now. She lets her next words tumble out in her familiar lilting tenor that for the past year, only the guts have heard.

"Naw. I knew." She finds Paul Clay's gaze and holds it like the reins of a wild horse. "That's why I put him in the ground."

One of his men whistles around a cackling whoop.

"She'd a rather killed her own man than go to bed with you," he hollers while the others take turns teasing him in kind.

Paul Clay's face darkens with fury.

"I ain't a piece of meat," Abilene cuts in, the shaking in her hands the only thing betraying her fear. "You can take my money, but yer gonna leave me be, y'hear? Or else I—"

He darts quicker than a rattler, seizing her arm before snapping the butt of his gun over her head. Her vision flashes red when she hits the ground, but she still manages to thrash and buck him away, teeth bared to bite and nails out to scratch as she tries to get at her gun. Even manages to pry it loose from her waistband before the other men converge on them. They kick her prone body before ripping her gun away.

In the shuffle, the bag of guts has fallen completely open. Through gathering tears and gasps for air, she gives the closest man an admirable shove that sends him tumbling into the pile.

"Ugh! What in Sam Hill—?" he cries, trying and failing to shuffle upright in the slick meaty globs.

The other men stop grappling with her to laugh at him, but Paul Clay won't be deterred. He catches her by the neck and starts to squeeze. She claws at his arms, pleas building and dying on her tongue.

"Ugly little bitch," he sneers. "Teach you to—"

Screams cut him off. Raw, rasping, many-throated shouts of terror and pain. Paul Clay's grip loosens, but he's on top of her now, knees on either side of her stomach with his full weight keeping her down. With effort, she cranes her neck toward the other men, her own ill fortune dissolving to nothing at the impossible, gruesome, horrifying sight.

The man who fell in the guts is now buried beneath them. A seething, charnel pool that splashes over his bearded face, pieces crawling into his open mouth to slide down his throat. The pile seems to grow, intestines unfurling like wildflower petals to strangle him.

The other men move slow, stupid with fear.

"What witchcraft is this?" one shouts, pointing his gun.

"Don't shoot!" says another. "You'll hit him."

They drop to the ground to tear at the living guts as an entranced Abilene watches from where Paul Clay's got her pinned.

"Hell's goin' on over there?" he snarls.

An earthquake. A pounding, rhythmic tremor under her back. A trickle of blood trails down her temple, heartbeats quickening to new levels of horror when she sees what's making the very world tremble.

Sunny gives a honking bray and backs to the far corner of his pen. The man suffocating in the intestinal pile gurgles once before going still, his buddies too preoccupied pulling up their guns toward the approaching...*thing* thundering toward them. Their horses—hitched to some posts by the dirt path—squeal in a deafening pitch, bucking and kicking to get loose.

Slowly, Paul Clay rises. Abilene wastes no time shuffling away from him. Ducking into the pen, gunshots and cries ringing in her ears, she allows herself a look at the creature. Such things can't be possible, but she knows, in the darkest crevasses of her soul, exactly what it is. The preserved guts from the magical valley, each and every one of them desirously held, caressed, and loved by her before finding their home there.

In the dull lantern light, the monster's infinite globular jewels gleam as they tumble and splat their way to the men who attacked her. Bullets strike, tearing pieces of it apart only to have them replaced by others. On the tarp, the guts slide off the dead man's purple corpse and writhe toward the giant beast. Toward home.

The men try to run. Try to scream. But in an instant, a tidal wave of offal crashes over them, tangling them inside. Cries become strangled wet moans. She hears their bones snap like kindling. Fresh blood oozes between the slithering viscera now hot on Paul Clay's heels.

He fires his gun til the blasts turn to clicks. The meat monster towers over him, his cronies' broken bodies abandoned behind it.

"No," he slurs, reaching for the sky. "No, please, I—"

The beast takes its time, dragging itself onto Paul Clay's ankles, individual chunks rolling up his legs, then his torso, trapping him in its pulsing crush til he can't get enough wind to keep begging. The guts leave his face exposed, like it wants Abilene to witness every second of Paul Clay's gruesome demise. His gaping jaw, trembling chapped lips, darting tongue, blue-tinged cheeks and veiny eyes bulging from their sockets.

And when the low-down bastard breathes his last, Abilene can't help the satisfied smile that near splits her face in half. When the monster comes rolling through the wooden fence for her, she's ready. Arms extended, unwilling to look away. The picture of surrender. She ain't afraid to die. Not like this.

Still, she can't help the single fearful mewl as the guts drag her inside their countless folds and climb the length of her body, burrowing under her clothes, sliding across her cheeks and parted mouth. The world blurs, Sunny's braying and the nickering horses muffled by the swarming press that holds her.

She registers in a faint, far-off way that they're moving, edging in a cascading river toward the gulch. The guts leave her enough room to breathe, a sensation like a slow hand stroking her back as if to tell her she's safe.

"I ain't scared," she assures the beast as she tumbles with it over the shallow cliff's edge and into its valley.

And she means it. She's never been held this way. Protected this way. *Loved* this way.

Nestled at the bottom of the ravine, wrapped in its silken cocoon, a trailing intestine skims her flickering pulse point. A question.

"Do it," she whispers, closing her eyes. The intestine coils rapturously around her throat, tightening as it goes. The guts deepen their smothering embrace, fitting around her better than any man ever could.

We got you, sweet Abilene. You ain't alone.

"*God almighty,*" she croaks through her thinning windpipe.

That we are, the monster—her beautiful, boundless flesh god—purrs as it tenderly drags her soul into its charnel heaven.

Above the gulch, a lone buzzard circles.

BAD WATER

DESIREE HORTON

"WHAT DOES THAT MEAN? BAD WATER?" Virginia asked.

"It means," Cecil said, pulling his hat off his head, releasing a cascade of dust in the fading light of the evening sun, "It'll make you sick. It's not clean."

"So, what? We'll need to cook it for a while longer? Put a piece of silver in it?"

Cecil gestured to the Native man walking away from them, his face a mask of concern. "Ol' chief over there is telling it otherwise."

Virginia, exhausted, was quickly losing patience with her brother-in-law's hesitancy to relay anything he considered bad news. It had taken him half a day to tell her of her husband's death. His own brother, for God's sake. They had been on the emigrant trail for two months now, and it seemed the end would never be in sight. She would spend the rest of her short, miserable life on an endless dusty trail of unwashed people, animal shit, and her constantly hat-wringing brother-in-law.

"Cecil, can you please speak plainly? I'd sooner know the position we're in and come up with a plan of action now, rather than next week when it becomes a problem," she said, her fingers massaging her eyes.

"Well, ma'am, he said there's bad water up ahead. But it's worse than bad water, it's... I don't know, evil water? I'm not sure I understood everything he said."

Virginia was surprised by how long Cecil had survived in this country on his own. Deep down, she doubted his claims entirely. He had written to his brother of this great land out west and had traveled east to meet them in Missouri. His letters had been full to bursting with exaltations of Willamette Valley, which still seemed as far away now as it had that day her husband decided they should join his brother in making their fortune out west. A fool's errand, clearly, but there was nothing to be done about it now. This was not a trip Virginia could make on her own, so she was stuck with Cecil, at least until they reached her destination. She could cry for Aaron later, and she would, but now she needed to focus on survival.

"So let me see if I understand," Virginia said. "We can take this shortcut with the 'bad water' and shave three weeks off our trip, potentially getting to Willamette Valley before the snow comes, or we can continue with the wagon train and probably lose the rest of our oxen in the journey. Did he tell you which river to avoid? Is it something we can go around? I thought you knew this trail. Did you have trouble with the water before?"

He reacted to her words like stones being pelted at him, wincing and flinching. Her eyes bored holes into him as she waited for a response. He gripped the edges of his hat and looked down at the ground.

"It's not *exactly* like that," he said weakly.

"What...do you *mean*," she said, her voice pure ice.

"I haven't taken this one myself, per se, but there's a very reliable guide who can meet us on the other side of the Snake River. Plus, the Woolbrights are taking the shortcut too, so we wouldn't be all on our own. They've left already but if we leave soon we should catch up with them by nightfall."

Virginia fought to remain calm with this new information. She wasn't surprised, but she was furious. She would give her right arm to be rid of Cecil right now, but it seemed like she would have to settle for a dangerous stretch of trail, bad water, and ending their tumultuous and brief relationship three weeks early. She wanted to scream, but instead, she took a deep breath, smoothed the front of her dress, and nodded.

"Okay, shortcut it is. I'll see if I can barter with one of the other families for some extra vinegar or something."

Cecil looked at her blankly.

"For the water. Vinegar for the water, Cecil."

His face lit up with understanding. "Oh, yes! Brilliant idea, Virginia. I told Aaron he picked a smart one."

That made Virginia's chest ache, and she turned away from Cecil, digging through the wagon for items to trade. When she turned back, he was thankfully gone, over speaking with the other family taking the shortcut, and Virginia could wipe the dust, definitely not tears, from her eyes. What was a little bad water if it meant being free of that imbecile three glorious weeks sooner?

The beeves groaned and huffed as they pulled forlornly toward the lake ahead of them. The skies had turned a brilliant red, backlighting the dark, dead trees around them like shadows around a fire. She pitied the animals, who were desperately thirsty and bone thin. She couldn't bear to hear their moans, though she wasn't fond of the creatures.

Cecil pulled them all to a halt and hopped down off the wagon. He eyed the lake warily. The water was dead calm, nary a ripple, as if neither bug nor fish would dare disturb the surface. Virginia was tired, dirty, and about three seconds from throttling Cecil.

"Is this it? The bad water the Indian was talking about?" she asked, easing her sore body from the seat and down toward the cracked earth. She thought it strange how unnourished the surrounding land seemed, with a perfectly good body of water right in front of them. Maybe it was the land that was bad. Was that possible?

Cecil stepped forward and dunked his hands in the water, pooling some in his palms and bringing it to his face cautiously. He gave it a sniff, then slurped up a bit and swished it around his mouth. Virginia watched him, one eyebrow raised expectantly. He swallowed and gave her a toothy grin that bordered on manic. For some reason, his reaction disturbed Virginia more than if he'd keeled over dead on the spot. She had never seen Cecil smile like that, teeth bared like a spooked animal.

"Tastes great!" He pushed his cupped hands toward her face. "Here, try some!"

Virginia pushed his hands away. "No, thank you, I'll take your word for it."

"He must have been talking about a different lake or something; this here seems about as good as spring water. We lucked out!"

The water dribbled out of Cecil's hands, leaving dark trails in the dirt down his arms that reminded Virginia of blood. The thought made her queasy. He began to unhitch the animals. Virginia looked around, still uneasy, though having trouble pinning down the reason. It wasn't until they had a campfire going and dinner beans bubbling in the pot that Virginia spoke again.

"Cecil."

Cecil, busy whittling a small piece of wood into a poor approximation of a bear, looked up at her. "Yes?"

"Where are the Woolbrights?"

Cecil stared at her uncomprehendingly. "Woolbrights?"

"Yes. They were ahead of us. Why aren't they camped here? We couldn't have been more than a day behind them. Why aren't they camped here by the lake?"

Cecil looked around them, as if they had merely overlooked them in the distance. After a minute, he shrugged. "Must have pushed off early. We'll catch them at the river."

"There are no tracks. If they came through here, we would have seen something. Wheel marks, oxen excrement, footprints. *Something*, Cecil. It doesn't look like anyone has come through here for quite some time. Why wouldn't they have stopped to at least fill up the barrels?"

Cecil looked around again, as if in their discussion of the Woolbrights, they would summon them in the darkness. He didn't look concerned, which was strange to Virginia. Cecil always looked concerned. The man was a perpetual quaking mess; why was he now so unconcerned? So *relaxed?* He looked back at his hands and began whittling again.

"Maybe they just aren't as smart as you, Virginia," he said cooly.

Virginia's jaw dropped. Cecil had never spoken to her like that before. She closed her mouth and frowned, resolving not to speak any more that night. They would be on their way in the morning, and she could figure things out then. She scooped some beans into a bowl and handed it to Cecil, who began to eat, ignoring the steam billowing from the surface. Her appetite vanished, so she sat and watched him eat. When he was finished, he licked the bowl with relish and stood abruptly.

"Gonna go give this a wash for ya. Might even give myself a bath while I'm down there," Cecil called over his shoulder, already walking away from the campfire.

Virginia was confounded. Cecil had never, in Virginia's six months of knowing him, offered to wash a single dish or voluntarily taken a bath. All bathing had been at the behest of his brother, and Virginia was pretty sure those went out the window when Aaron passed.

Something was not right with Cecil. Virginia felt like an animal with its hackles raised, unable to shake the feeling of *wrongness*. She sat by the fire, listening to the silence around them. Unnatural silence. No bugs chirping, no coyotes or wolves howling, not so much as a crunch of a twig from a creature in the darkness. Just silence.

And then laughter.

Unable to suppress a shiver, Virginia listened to the sound of splashing and giggling, as if Cecil was having himself a grand old time down at the lake. Alone. In the dark. Virginia wondered briefly if the fool could even swim. How deep was this lake? Cecil had led the animals over to be watered when they arrived. The creatures had bellowed and lowed, drank deeply, then lay down on the banks to nap. She, herself, had not yet ventured down to it. As lovely as a bath sounded, or a cool drink of water, she couldn't get rid of the ache in her gut every time she thought about taking a sip, instead choosing to finish off the dregs of their water barrel. She knew they would need to refill it soon, but every time she thought about hauling the barrel down to the lake and filling it full, she wanted to scream. She was unused to this kind of vague fear taking over her. Thus far in their trip, she had been almost unflappable. Now this seeming oasis was giving her the vapors.

Virginia lay out her bedroll, ignoring the hoots and hollers coming from Cecil, who sounded as if he were a one-man band with all that racket. Absurdly joyous, with a hint of what Virginia could only describe as menace. She lay down as close to the fire as she dared and fell asleep dreaming of a steaming hot bath back in the home she'd shared with Aaron months ago. The cracked ground soaked up her tears with a fury she did not see.

Virginia woke to a red sky, the same shade it had been when they arrived last night. Disoriented, she sat up and looked around, the blood-red hue staining the ground around her a dusky scarlet.

Something was wrong.

The fire was out.

Cecil was gone.

Her chest heaved as she realized the wagon was gone too. Where were the animals? She jumped up from her bedroll, walking in circles around the extinguished fire, the only thing to see for miles except the skeletons of trees and the lake. With trepidation, Virginia trudged to the water's edge. She tried to contain the panic that was building like steam in a cook pot.

She could see wagon tracks, and about 20 feet away, something white, making the barest of ripples at the water's surface. Her heart sank. The wagon canvas. Her wagon was at the bottom of this lake. *The animals? Were they in the lake too?* She stopped short of the lake's edge, her toes curling away from that placid body of water.

Where was Cecil?

"Cecil!" she called, her voice cracked and dry. "Cecil! We need to get moving!" She felt silly lying. Where would they go with the wagon in the water? Perhaps they could pull it out? Could she salvage anything inside? There was no answer, her voice drifting away from her and getting stuck in the sky, which pressed in on her claustrophobically.

"Cecil, please," she choked, tears pricking the edges of her eyes. "Something's wrong!"

She looked back at her bedroll, unsure of what to do. There was no plan for this, no pioneer spirit to see her through. Cecil was gone. Aaron, long gone, his body broken in a hunting accident only a month into their journey, and half a year into their ill-fated marriage. She had no family behind her and nothing ahead of her. She had no idea where she was, perhaps somewhere in Utah?

She thought back to Cecil's strange behavior, the splashing and shouting. *Oh god, that idiot DID drown?* Filled with terror at the thought of being truly alone, she splashed into the water, desperate to see one way or the other.

She swam, her dress pulling at her, beckoning her down, down,

down to the bottom. As she pulled herself forward toward the lake's center, she had to admit how refreshing it felt. The water was cool and seemed to hold back the sky, which pressed in on her even now, threatening to smother her. It sparkled silver over her hands as she paddled, and she found herself slowing down to admire it, before remembering what she was doing and resuming her paddling.

When she reached the center of the lake, she gazed around, looking for a landmark or anything to keep her oriented. Then she took a deep breath and dived down.

Dusky and blue, it was like a different world under the surface, beautiful and weightless. She kept her eyes open as she swam down, looking for the bottom of the lake, knowing there would be clues for her there.

And there were.

They were all there. Her dress settled her down on the lake bottom, like gentle wings, and there she saw Cecil. He wasn't alone. Aaron was there too, and the animals. A crowd of other smiling people she recognized, even the Woolbrights, waiting to greet her. She felt like a great weight had been lifted off her shoulders. The hard part was done. She only needed to let go of the breath she was holding and settle here with them. Pioneers of this watery land, not the first and certainly not the last. She felt Aaron's hand touch hers. She turned toward him, ready to empty her lungs, ready to stay here with him.

Instead, Cecil grasped her hand in his, smiling maniacally, every tooth showing bright in the glittering sunbeams that reached the lake floor, and the breath Virginia was holding came out as a scream.

NOOSE CREEK

AN AGGIE ADVENTURE
D.L. WINCHESTER

South Dakota
1879

AGGIE AND ROCHE rode into the dusty town as the sun was setting.

"You okay?" Aggie asked, noticing her father's wince.

"Yeah, I'm fine," he replied, but she knew he wasn't. Six months in a military infirmary had healed his wounds, but he was still adjusting to the rigors of life on the trail. They'd taken it slow across northern Wyoming, but when they saw this town on the horizon, Roche had insisted they could make it before nightfall.

Aggie hadn't thought her father was ready, but she knew he didn't want to appear weak to her. She'd spent six months nursing him back to health after two of his former soldiers had left him for dead outside the Hole-in-the-Wall. He was trying to make up for her seeing him at his weakest, she knew.

Aggie had let him, even though he didn't have to impress her.

Fighting back from death's door had done that.

The main street looked thrown together, wooden buildings on either side of a rough dirt street. If any rain fell, it'd be less a street and more a giant mud puddle.

"Would you look at that," Roche said, pointing to one of the windows.

Aggie looked over and saw the body of a white-haired man in a casket, propped up for anyone passing by to pay their respects.

"Yeah, so?"

Roche swung off his horse and led it to a hitching post. Aggie did the same, following her father as he limped toward the window. Getting him walking had been the hardest part of his recovery, but the surgeon hoped the limp would become less noticeable over time.

"He's been embalmed," Roche said, studying the man in the coffin.

"What?" Aggie asked.

"They preserved him," Roche explained. "Some folks had it done when their loved ones died in the war, to get them home for burial. But it really took off when they did it to President Lincoln. His funeral train took two weeks to go from Washington to Illinois, and his body was viewed by thousands."

"And he didn't stink?" Aggie asked, thinking of her hometown of Ojinaga, Mexico. In the heat, you had to get a body buried quick, or the smell would dominate the funeral.

Roche shook his head. "That's the thing about it. They replace the blood with chemicals, and it stops decomposition."

"Must be expensive," Aggie said.

Roche shrugged. "Probably. The last time I saw it personally was President Lincoln. Stood in line for six hours to pay my respects. I sure didn't figure I'd see it in rural South Dakota."

The door to the building opened, and a man in a brown apron came out. He had long brown hair pulled back in a ponytail and dark eyes. "I saw you admiring my handiwork," he said, gesturing at the coffin.

"I was," Roche replied. "It's been a while since I've seen an embalmed body."

"He looks like he could wake up and step through that window," Aggie added.

The man smiled. "Thank you for saying so. It's an art I learned back in the east. When I decided to come west, I brought it with me. In this climate, having a little extra time to say farewell can be a blessing." His grin became wider. "And of course, if someone passes in the winter, it helps ease the odor until the ground thaws."

"Naturally," Roche said.

"Until the ground thaws?" Aggie asked.

The man turned to her. "I take it you're not from a northern climate?"

Aggie shook her head. "Mexico."

"Well, up here in the Dakotas, the extreme cold causes the ground to freeze, making it almost impossible to dig a grave during the winter months," he explained. For some reason, Aggie found the perfection of his diction to be annoying. "So we have to wait until the ground thaws in the spring to bury folks. In most cases, the cold helps keep the odor down, but sometimes the ground doesn't thaw as fast as the decedents do."

"Makes sense," Aggie said. "So what does embalming entail?"

He put a finger to his lips. "I'm afraid that's a trade secret. At any rate, it's nothing to discuss with a lady such as yourself."

Aggie opened her mouth to protest the accusation, but Roche cut her off. "So everyone has their own way of doing it?"

"The principles are the same, but there are small differences in technique that separate the gifted from the average."

"I didn't catch your name," Roche said.

"Thomas Alexander, at your service." The man extended a hand, and Roche took it.

"Folks call me Roche. This here's Aggie."

Aggie nodded to him.

"I'd love to buy you a drink, perhaps hear more about your craft," Roche said.

"Unfortunately, I am already engaged for the evening, but I appreciate the offer."

"Ah, well, perhaps another time."

"Perhaps," Alexander replied. "If you'll excuse me, I must get back to work."

"That's fine." Roche smiled as Alexander went back inside.

"What the hell was that about?" Aggie asked as they led their horses away.

"Embalming?"

"No, that 'nothing to discuss with a lady' bullshit!"

Roche smiled. "It ain't personal. I know you're strong enough to handle anything, but sometimes it's good if folks don't know that. Being underestimated can be an advantage."

"Like with your limp?" she replied, nodding toward his leg.

A pause, then a nod. "I suppose. Let's get these horses to the livery stable, then find the hotel."

After they got settled in at the hotel, Roche left his daughter to rest while he headed next door to the Aces Saloon. He'd agreed to form a bounty hunting partnership with Aggie—now he just needed to find someone for them to track down.

As he'd hoped, a lawman was sitting at the bar. Roche sat down next to him and ordered a drink. When the bartender walked away, he turned to the lawman.

"Howdy."

The lawman looked up from his drink, and Roche saw his badge read "Sheriff."

"Hello, stranger."

"Name's Roche." Roche stuck out a hand, and the sheriff took it.

"Bill Barber. What brings you to Noose Creek?"

"Noose Creek?" Roche asked.

Barber shrugged. "Apparently one of the first civic functions around here was a hanging, and the name stuck."

"Ah. Well, I'm a bounty hunter looking for work."

Barber nodded. "I've got a stack of wanted dodgers at my office. You're welcome to come down tomorrow and take a look."

The barman sat Roche's drink in front of him, and he took a sip. "Anything close?"

Barber shrugged. "Criminals don't exactly like to advertise their whereabouts, you know."

"I reckon that's true." Roche took another sip, then gestured the bartender for another round.

"I do have some questions about that new undertaker though," Barber said.

"Thomas Alexander?"

A nod. "He's only been here a couple months, but we've already had six funerals. Seven, if you count Cliff Hynes's tomorrow. I been here three years, and I can count on one hand the funerals we had before Alexander got here. That's counting the two fools who shot each other one high noon."

"You think he's making his own business?" Roche asked.

Barber shrugged again. "Maybe. Can't prove nothin'. It's mostly just creepy, the way he props them up in the window. I can't walk to my office without feelin' like they're looking at me."

Roche smiled. "I saw that as I came into town."

"Ol' Cliff wouldn't've liked being the center of attention like that. Or being dressed up in those fancy duds." The sheriff finished off his drink as the bartender sat the next one in front of him. "But that Alexander fellow talked Delia Hynes into it." The sheriff shuddered. "That ain't even mentioning what someone with his talent is doing in Noose Creek. We're the ends of the earth, and we got an undertaker who makes dead folk look lifelike? It don't make a lot of sense."

Roche nodded. "I see what you mean." He finished his drink and sat the glass on the bar. "I'll swing by tomorrow, take a look at those wanted dodgers if that's okay."

"Sounds fine." The sheriff held up his glass. "Thanks for the drink."

Roche opened the door to his room and realized someone was sitting on the bed. His hand went to his gun.

"Don't think I'd try that, Roche."

He sighed "Damn it, Aggie."

She chuckled. "I learned a few tricks in the brothel. Picking locks is just one of them."

"What brothel?" Roche asked, finding the lamp and lighting it. He'd gone nineteen years without his daughter in his life, and though they'd had six months to catch up, there was still a lot of their pasts they hadn't shared.

"The one in Dodge City I worked at while I was saving up to come looking for you," she replied. "I was the cleaning lady. Your soldier friends didn't feel comfortable giving me a more 'active' job."

He chuckled. "Sounds about right."

"You go looking for that undertaker?"

A shake of the head. "The sheriff, actually. I was trying to find us some work."

"And?"

"He don't like the undertaker."

"Wasn't a fan of him myself," Aggie replied.

"The sheriff said he's been here a couple months, and the death rate has skyrocketed."

"So what are we gonna do?"

Roche shrugged. "Look into it, I guess."

Roche and Aggie walked downstairs for breakfast the next morning to find the sheriff waiting in the lobby.

"You didn't tell me you had a woman," Barber said, standing.

"Ain't my woman," Roche said with a smile. "This is my daughter, Aggie."

A nod from the sheriff. "Howdy, ma'am."

Aggie nodded back.

"I wasn't sure I'd made such a strong impression," Roche said.

"Well, I can be a little standoffish when I drink," Barber explained. "I sobered up real quick when I heard LouAnn Glenn passed this morning."

"Eight," Roche replied.

"That's right," the sheriff said. "I can't help but think something's up, but I ain't much good for investigating—they all know me, won't talk straight if I ask questions. The only reason I'm sheriff is no one else wanted it, and this town ain't big enough for two barbers."

Roche laughed. "Sounds about right."

"What's the pay?" Aggie asked.

The sheriff looked at her, then smiled. "You get right to the point, don't you?"

Aggie nodded.

"Can't pay much. Hell, the town won't even hire me a deputy. But I reckon I can swing a dollar a day, plus any reward money you pick up along the way."

"That's for each of us?" Roche asked.

"Her too?"

"We're a team," Roche explained.

He shook his head. "Ain't never heard of a woman bounty hunter."

"Neither had the two men who left me for dead six months ago," Roche replied. "Folks don't expect Aggie."

"She any good?" Barber asked.

"I spent twenty years in the army," Roche replied. "I'd put her up against any man I served with in a shooting contest."

"There's more to being a bounty hunter than shooting," the sheriff pointed out.

A nod. "That ain't a lie. But she's a quick learner."

"Well, hell. Then you're both hired."

That night, Aggie found herself in the alley behind Alexander's shop. They'd spent the morning looking at wanted dodgers in the sheriff's office before Roche sent her back to the hotel for a nap.

Now she was staring at the back door, wondering what she'd find inside.

"This guy seems to have come out of nowhere," Roche told her before she left. "I ain't sure what you're gonna find, but I reckon you're looking for something that suggests he ain't what he says he is."

Aggie tried the door.

Unlocked.

"Shit," she muttered. Not a sign of someone with something to hide.

She slipped inside, waiting for her eyes to adjust to the darkness. The back room had high windows on the wall facing the alley, letting some moonlight in. Aggie stood for a moment, looking around.

Toward the center of the room was a large table. She stepped closer to see what was on it...

"Fuck!"

A dead woman lay on the table.

Aggie wasn't bothered by dead folk, but she hadn't been expecting company while she searched. The woman wasn't covered or anything, just lying naked, face up, with something sticking an inch or so out of her chest.

There was a desk against the far wall, and Aggie went to it. The top was clean, so she started opening drawers, digging through them in the dark until, in the bottom drawer, she found a stack of letters. She stuck them in her shirt, intending to go through them later. The paper of the envelope felt cool against her bare skin.

Now she had to decide. There wasn't much else she could see without better lighting, but if she lit a lamp, someone could see the light through the windows.

She closed the drawer and stood up. She'd start with the letters, and if she needed to come back, she'd ask Roche if he had any ideas for the light problem.

Aggie walked toward the alley door, but before she got there, she heard footsteps outside.

She looked around and saw a closet. She opened the door and slipped inside as the back door swung open.

There were footsteps, then a sliver of light showed near her feet.

"Didn't plan for this one," a voice muttered. "Old woman just croaked."

It sounded like Alexander, but far less polished than when he'd been talking to Roche. He had an accent too, one Aggie wasn't sure she'd ever heard before.

There was a thump, followed by another a few moments later.

"Another embalming," he muttered to himself.

Aggie peeked through a crack in the door to see him pouring liquid from bottles into a large tank. A different woman was on the table now, smaller than the other one. Aggie couldn't see where the bigger woman was now. "Have to order more soon," he sat the bottle on the counter. "Half my last order broke on the trip out here."

Alexander looked down at the body and sighed. "I hate to let blood go to waste."

Leaning over the table, he bit into the woman's neck.

Aggie gasped. Was he sucking the dead woman's blood?

What the hell?

Alexander continued for several minutes before finally standing up. He wiped a trickle of blood on his sleeve, then reached for the brown apron he'd worn when he was talking to Roche and Aggie earlier. Putting it on, he picked up a scalpel and made an incision in the woman's neck. After working a few moments, he took a tube connected to a tank and attached something to the end before inserting it into the opening.

He picked up a rubber bulb and began squeezing it. Through the tube, she could see fluid running from the tank into the body. Something started dripping, and Aggie saw fluid draining off the table into a bucket.

What the hell was embalming? From what she could see it didn't look natural at all.

It was fascinating, yet macabre, Aggie decided as the smell of blood reached her. That had to be what was flowing into the bucket under the table, as the fluid in the tank replaced what was left of the woman's blood after Alexander fed.

She wanted to get out of here, but she couldn't leave the closet without Alexander seeing her. After a while, the tank was empty, and Aggie hoped he would leave. Instead, he wheeled a coffin into view, and Aggie realized that's where he'd put the other woman. He began to dress her, laying clothing over her and tucking it around her, securing it with a needle and thread.

Suddenly, he walked toward the closet.

"Shit!" Aggie thought. Where the fuck was Roche? He was supposed to be keeping a lookout. Alexander was reaching for the handle when she heard the crash of glass from the front room.

"What the hell?" Alexander turned and moved toward the sound. Aggie didn't hesitate, leaving the closet and dashing out the back door.

The next morning, Roche looked at the letters Aggie found and shook his head. "Only language I know is English, and these ain't written in English." He handed her one. "This alphabet ain't even right. Look at those letters."

Aggie studied them a moment. There were some letters she recognized, but some she'd definitely never seen before. "So we don't know anything."

He held up the envelopes the letters had come in. "We know he was writing to someone in Philadelphia. And if the embalming fluid fumes weren't messing with your mind, we know Alexander likes the taste of blood."

"All I smelled was blood," Aggie said. "But Alexander works closely with those chemicals all the time, so maybe the fumes messed with his mind and made him think he's a vampire."

"Or he actually is one." Roche had been the first to use the term, but Aggie had picked it up quickly. "That'd explain all the deaths since he arrived, him feeding." He sighed. "I ain't fully up to date with vampire lore, but I thought if one bit you, you turned into a vampire. But he's putting these folks in caskets, and they're staying there. Otherwise, there'd be a lot more bloodsuckers around."

"How do you kill a vampire?" Aggie asked.

"You drive a stake through its heart," Roche replied. "That much I remember."

Aggie thought about the thing sticking out of the woman's chest. "That's what Alexander does. He feeds, which turns them, then he immediately kills them."

Roche nodded. "That'd be one way to do it. He probably figures there's only room for one vampire in a town this small."

"So what do we do?" Aggie asked. "Tell the sheriff?"

A laugh. "How do you figure that conversation will go?"

She paused, then sighed. "Right."

"The first thing we need to do is return these letters," Roche said, holding them up. "Then we wait for our opportunity." He looked out the window, and a confused look crossed his features.

"What's wrong?" Aggie asked.

"I don't know much about vampires, but I know they shouldn't be able to stroll down a street at high noon."

Aggie joined him at the window, watching as Alexander disappeared into a shop down the street.

"Maybe you're wrong?"

Roche shook his head. "There were a couple Slavic boys in my regiment once, liked to tell stories about creatures from the homeland. They were damn clear—vampires don't survive in the sun."

Aggie shrugged. "Maybe he isn't a vampire."

Roche shrugged too. "We'll get those letters back tonight, and go from there."

Well after dark, Aggie left the hotel and made her way to the alley outside the undertaker's shop. The front window had been covered by boards where Roche had broken it the night before.

She tried the door, and found it was still unlocked. She slipped inside. It took a moment for her eyes to adjust to the dark, but as soon as they did, she made her way past the embalming table to the desk. Kneeling, she opened the bottom drawer and placed the letters inside.

The room lit up, and Aggie turned to see Alexander next to a lamp.

"I wondered who took my letters," he said, stepping between Aggie and the door, raising a pistol and pointing it at her. "Not that I think you learned anything, with them being written in Russian."

"We made some educated guesses," Aggie said, looking at the gun.

Alexander followed her gaze and laughed. "I'm sure you're tempted to try to cut me down, but even if you manage to squeeze off a round, it won't harm me." His tone was mixed, a combination of his formal voice and the casual phrasing she'd heard the night before.

"Because you're a vampire," Aggie said.

Alexander nodded. "Very good, very good. Yes, I was bitten as a boy in Vladivostok. Naturally, I had to learn to hide my true nature from the world. I fed on the blood of animals, goats and sheep mostly, the occasional stray dog."

"Dog," Aggie muttered. "I guess you are what you eat."

Alexander's mouth dropped open, then he chuckled. "A joke. Clever. I was ten when my father heard of a man in Moscow who worked with children like me, and sent me to live with him. There, I didn't have to hide my peculiarity, and was able to embrace my true self. In a city of thousands, no one cared if the odd urchin or panhandler went missing. I learned to feast!

"Then, a tragic mistake. One of us consumed the child of a duke. We fled Moscow, landing in America. Here, we learned to embalm as the art gained popularity. Since then, we've spread out across the nation, able to live comfortably and provide a service to the public."

"You drink blood!" Aggie protested.

"Blood that would go to waste if not for us," Alexander replied.

"Waste? You're murdering them to meet your own needs!"

"They would die anyway. Perhaps not as fast, but as miserable as life is here, I like to think of it as part of my service. I prey on the old, infirm, and downtrodden, those whose deaths aren't likely to seem suspicious."

"How do you keep from getting burned in the sunlight?" Aggie asked, changing the subject. He seemed to have forgotten the pistol in his hand, and she wanted to keep it that way. Hopefully Roche would realize something was wrong, and come to save her.

Again.

Alexander reached inside his shirt with his non-gun hand and took out a silver amulet with a purple stone in the center. "My mentor developed this, to protect us from sunlight.

"Interesting," Aggie said.

Behind Alexander, the door to the alley opened, and Roche slipped inside.

"Enough talk!" Alexander said. "Young, fresh blood is a luxury, and tonight I will feast!"

As Alexander stepped toward Aggie, Roche charged, raising his arm and thrusting. A moment later, Aggie saw the blood-covered tip of a wooden stake emerge through Alexander's chest.

The vampire stood a moment, looking down at the stake sticking out of him. The gun slipped from his fingers and clattered to the floor. A moment later, Alexander collapsed, disappearing into a pile of dust before his body could hit the ground.

All that was left was a pile of clothes and the amulet.

Aggie picked up the amulet and held it out to Roche. "He said his mentor developed it, to protect them from the sun."

"I know, I was listening at the door the whole time."

She chuckled. "I wish I'd known that. I was scared to death you weren't going to show up."

"If you'd known I was there, you'd have acted different, tipped him off," Roche explained. "You were never in danger, I just had to wait for the right opportunity."

Aggie rolled her eyes. "That's easy for you to say. You weren't the one he was pointing a gun at!"

The next morning, they rode east, leaving Noose Creek behind. Each of them had two silver dollars in their pockets.

"You think we should have told the sheriff about the others?"

Roche shrugged. "They ain't exactly his problem. And if he tried to warn other folks about them, they'd just think he's crazy."

"So we take down Alexander and call it a day?"

Roche smiled. "You can't rid the world of evil. But you can deal with what's in front of you."

"I don't know that I like that," Aggie said.

"I know I don't like it," Roche replied. "But you learn to live with it. Or it drives you crazy. Neither option changes the amount of evil you can deal with."

"So we do what we can, then ride off to the next town?"

"Something like that," Roche said.

Aggie shook her head, then spurred her horse into a trot, wondering what kind of evil they'd face next.

THE HUNGERS

MADI HAAB

THE REMAINS of Luisa's dream scattered at the sight of the dead heifer.

Pa was hard at work cleaning it up. He'd clearly been up for a while now, but he hadn't roused her even though the sun was already peering above the distant hills.

Luisa rushed down the porch stairs. "Pa? What happened?"

His eyes widened with something close to horror, like she'd just caught him red handed. "I got it, honey. Stay back," he said, but she was already close enough to see the carcass.

Her hand flew to her mouth.

The heifer's flank was pockmarked with strange divots; the image of worms tunneling in the flesh of an apple wriggled into Luisa's mind, except these would have to be the size of rattlesnakes. Too late to save the meat. They might render the tallow, but the hide couldn't be sold: muscles and ribs were bared, and the spill of its organs now baked in the sun.

"What...what *did* that?"

Pa took off his hat and ran a hand over his balding head. "Coyotes or something, I guess," he said without much conviction.

"But—"

"Didn't I just tell you to stay back?" he snapped, then winced. Luisa's heart fluttered, rabbit quick. "Sorry, honey. This is just ..." He lifted one hand and dropped it again.

"It's fine," Luisa said, forcing a smile. The ranch had been struggling since several of the cattle took sick last year, so she knew how upset he was. Through the cloud of flies, she saw one of the fence posts had toppled, and a few cows had scattered in the plains. "I'll bring back the others."

She returned inside to get dressed and braid her hair; it was damp, like she'd sweated through her sleep, though the nights were still chilly. Her stomach clenched with hunger, but she felt nauseous just thinking about eating, so after a cursory glance at the contents of the pantry, she headed for the stables.

She found a rusted metal basin overturned in a patch of wet grass outside, and returned it to its spot by the barn. The fading dream bloomed in her mind fleetingly: she'd been a small child again instead of fifteen, and her mother was still alive, lathering her in a basin just like this one while singing to her in Spanish. She'd poured water through Luisa's hair and rinsed the suds off her skin, careful not to get soap in her eyes; her smile and the timbre of her voice had been as crisp as the first bite of an apple, but now the memory had whittled down to a thick fall of black hair, pale hands, and the smell of wild thyme.

Luisa let go of the dream and the tender ache behind her breastbone. She saddled her favourite mare, Tilly, who nuzzled at her hand looking for carrots. "No treats just yet, girl," she whispered, patting Tilly's forehead. "We've got work to do."

She slung a coil of rope on her shoulder, hauled herself up onto the saddle, and lowered her hat over her brow. Then she rode out into the plains, which shone gold in the morning light.

"There you are, girl," Miss Burnett called. She was bottle-feeding an escaped calf that had wound up in her orchard. "Found this little one nibbling my nectarines this morning."

Luisa dismounted. "I'm so sorry, Miss Burnett." The calf had no intention of interrupting his drink, so she pulled off one buckskin glove and stroked his back. Luisa's gaze tripped on her own grimy fingernails, but Miss Burnett didn't notice her falter.

"Something got to our cows during the night," she continued, repressing a shudder at the memory of the strange holes bored into the carcass. "We lost a heifer."

"Oh, your poor pa. This is just rotten luck, isn't it?"

Luisa nodded. "Did you notice anything unusual last night?"

"I'm sorry, I didn't," Miss Burnett said, shaking her head. "Though there have been rumors of a creature that feeds on live-stock. Attacks them and drinks their blood. I've heard it called 'chupacabra'." She tilted her head. "Your mother never told you about it?"

"No, never," Luisa said.

Miss Burnett made a thoughtful noise. "Probably didn't want to scare you. You were still so little when she passed." The bottle now empty, she straightened up and stretched. "Whatever it is, you and your pa be careful."

"Thank you, Miss Burnett. And thanks for looking after our escapee here."

The calf looked up at her, chin dripping with milk. Miss Burnett scratched his forehead. Luisa took him and Tilly home with a basket of fresh nectarines so ripe the scent tickled her nose. She was ravenous after riding across the plains all day on an empty stomach; she ate until the sweet, juicy flesh suddenly made her queasy, and she threw her half-eaten fruit in the grass, somehow still unsated.

The way home was slow, what with the basket and leashed calf, and as she rode past Mr. Wilson's farm, she decided to talk to him. Pa had always told her to give the man a wide berth: the two of them had hated each other for as long as she could remember, but if Mr. Wilson had seen something, it was worth risking her father's ire.

She secured Tilly and the calf to a post, then crossed Mr. Wilson's cornfield, where he was driving his plow. "Good day, Mr. Wilson," she called out. He stared at her without stopping, so she had to lope next to him to stay apace. "We, um...we lost a head last night."

He frowned under the brim of his hat. "You accusing me, girl?"

Luisa's courage faltered. "No. *No.* It was probably just coyotes or wild dogs or—" *Chupacabras*, a voice at the back of her head supplied. "I just wondered if you'd seen or heard anything strange."

He snorted, then spat on the ground. "Just you."

Luisa was starting to see why Pa had warned her about him. "Why do you hate us so much?" she asked, voice shaking.

Mr. Wilson stopped his horses to better look at her, his mouth a contemptuous twist. He could have been handsome, with his square jaw and suntan, but the ugliness inside him seeped all the way through his exterior. "Why don't you ask your pa to tell you about your mother, huh?"

Then he gave his horses a switch and left her to stare at the moving plow, her mouth acid with anger.

By the time she got back home, the enclosure had been repaired and the heifer's carcass cleaned up. Her father sat on the porch, rolling tobacco in a sheet of corn husk. She could count on one hand the number of times she'd seen him smoke. His eyes were lined and tired, and her heart squeezed knowing all he'd lost and grieved.

"Miss Burnett gave us some nectarines," she said, holding the basket out to him. He glanced at its contents, then returned his attention to his cigarette. Not hungry either, then. "Pa?"

"Hm?"

"I spoke to Mr. Wilson."

His hands stilled. "You *what?*"

Luisa resisted the urge to cower. She stood there instead, holding her spine straight. "He said I should ask you about Mami."

Pain momentarily contorted his features; the corn husk started shaking in his fingers, sprinkling tobacco to the boards at his feet. "That bastard," Pa said, his voice whipping through the heat. A horse whinnied nearby. "You stay away from him, got it?"

"Yes, Pa. I'm sorry," Luisa said, but she knew he wasn't angry. He was *scared*. She took a breath. "Will you tell me about Mami, though?"

His jaw worked, a muscle twitching in the lengthening shadows. For a moment she thought he'd send her to her room, but he sighed as he seemingly came to a decision. "Suppose you're old enough to hear the truth now," he said, then put the half-rolled cigarette on the table next to him and rubbed his eyes. "I ain't got proof, but"—he cleared his throat—"I think he's responsible for your mother's death."

Heat rushed to her face. "*What?*"

"Could never get it out of him, but has to be. She...she sleep-walked, you know. Must've wandered on his property and startled him. He hated her, anyway. Bet he's pleased."

Luisa's chest heaved with a deep, shuddering breath. "Oh my God, Pa. Did he...did he *shoot* her?"

He nodded once, almost imperceptibly. She pressed one hand to her mouth. They'd told her it was an accident: a bad fall from her horse, though now Luisa wasn't sure if that was what she'd been told or what her grieving young mind had pictured. But knowing the truth felt like losing her all over again.

Scalding tears streamed down her face. She sat down hard on the chair next to her father; he drew her close and stroked her hair. "It's all right, honey," he whispered, rocking her against him. "I'll look after you just as well as she would have."

As the sun sank behind the hills, Luisa's sobs finally ebbed away. "I wish she were here," she said into the wet collar of his shirt.

He kissed the top of her head. "Me too, honey. Me too."

She'd cried herself to exhaustion, but still made the effort to draw water from the well to scrub her hands and rinse her face. Then she looked through their pantry: she'd barely eaten all day, so she forced herself to eat a few strips of jerky and a handful of dried fruit, then readied herself for bed. A pale round moon hung outside, silvering the rippling grass and the backs of their animals. She could just hear the porch creaking under her father's footsteps as he paced.

Below her window, something whispered her name.

Luisa.

The hairs rose on her nape. Luisa ran to bed and slipped under the covers, but every time she closed her eyes, she imagined Miss Burnett's chupacabra: in her mind, it was a gaunt, hairless thing, creeping in the dirt, drawing closer and closer.

She dreamed of her mother again that night. In the dream, Luisa had been wearing her mother's red dress, the one she'd been buried in, and her mother helped her take it off, gathering the circle skirt and slipping the off-the-shoulder bodice over her head. She slid the pendant earrings off her lobes and gently removed Luisa's makeup, the white handkerchief coming off her mouth stained with crimson.

Then she gave Luisa a sponge bath like she was still a little girl, and dressed her in a clean nightgown. "Don't let your father see," her mother said, and before Luisa could ask why, she woke up.

He must've let her sleep, because her bedroom was bathed in sunlight. Voices drifted up from the first floor; she sat up, wide awake, dreading the news of another dead cow. She wrapped herself in a housecoat and tried to let herself out of the room.

The door was locked.

She shook the knob. "Pa? *Pa!*" she called out, rapping her fist on the door.

The voices quieted down. Footsteps echoed up the stairs, then the hallway, soon followed by the key turning in the lock.

Pa opened the door. "Sorry, honey. Just...just a precaution."

He'd never locked her door before, but she supposed it was understandable given the circumstances. She shuddered, picturing the chupacabra slinking up the stairs to her bedroom, then remembered her mother's sleepwalking and wondered if the same could happen to her. What if she'd been outside, asleep, while some creature tore the heifer open?

What if it had killed her instead?

Luisa forced herself to breathe through the surge of panic. "Who's that downstairs?" she asked.

"Sheriff Sutton."

As if on cue, Sutton called out from below. "You know, I wouldn't mind asking Luisa a couple of questions while I'm here."

Pa shot her a look she couldn't read, then made his way back downstairs. Luisa, still barefoot, followed him. "Is everything alright, Mr. Sutton? Did you find out who did it?"

"Did what?" Sutton asked innocently, smoothing his moustache with two fingers.

She had the unpleasant feeling she was being tested; she looked at her father, who was frowning at the basket of nectarines on the table, then back at the star glinting on the sheriff's vest. "Killed our cow."

"Ah. Your pa was just telling me about that, but no. Luisa, Mr. Wilson was found dead this morning."

He might as well have dumped a pail of water on her head. Luisa instinctively drew closer to Pa. "Dead...dead how?"

"From what your pa told me, pretty much like how your cow died."

Luisa felt nauseous. No one deserved that—though if anyone

did, it was Mr. Wilson. "I haven't seen or heard anything," she said, choosing her words carefully. "I went to bed early and only just woke up."

Sutton smiled amiably, but she sensed danger. "Speaking of, sir, why the lock on your daughter's bedroom door?"

He'd asked her father, but Luisa couldn't stop herself: "If it was the same thing that killed our heifer, then you know he can't have done it," she said with a sidelong glance in her father's direction. "No one—no *human*—could have done that."

"I'm not accusing anyone yet," Sutton replied, "but it's my job to look into all possibilities, and there was some bad blood between Mr. Wilson and—"

"Bad blood? Mr. Wilson killed my mother. Were you ever going to do something about *that?*"

The outburst startled the two men; Sutton blinked at her, and Pa put a placating hand on her shoulder. "Not now, honey," he said, a warning in his eyes.

"But he—"

"Luisa, *enough*," he said, shooting her another look before turning back to Sutton. Luisa clenched her jaw shut and stared defiantly at the sheriff, nostrils flared. "I'm so sorry, Sheriff, I don't know what's gotten into her."

"No harm done. No child should lose her mother that young," Sutton said. He'd recovered from his surprise, but there was a new stiffness to his posture. "But maybe it'll be easier on her if you just come back to town with me. I'd like you to tell me again about last night."

Sutton clasped Pa's shoulder as he spoke. To her horror, her father let himself be led toward the door. "You can't *do* that," Luisa cried. "He didn't do anything."

"Then I won't be keeping him for long," Sutton said pleasantly. He looked at her one last time and shook his head. "You're the spitting image of your mother, God keep her."

Pa didn't come back that night. Luisa thought about telling Sutton everything she knew, but he'd think her mad or laugh her out of town if she started rambling about chupacabras. Besides, she didn't want to leave the herd alone.

If she caught who—or *what*—did it, then Sutton would have no choice but to let Pa go.

Come nighttime, she stood on the porch in her suede split skirt, holding her father's rifle. Hunger pangs twisted her stomach, but the sourdough biscuits she'd forced herself to eat only made her feel vaguely ill. At least the discomfort helped keep her awake as the night deepened.

The waning moon drew its slow arc in the sky. No sound but the snorts of sleeping beasts and the wind rippling the grass stretching in all directions. She didn't dare wander too far, but she drew a slow loop around the house when she felt herself getting drowsy, and—

Her heart jumped into her mouth. A long dark streak stained the back wall, from the foundation to the open window of her bedroom on the second floor.

Blood.

"No," she gasped. Fear gripped her throat, but she took deep breaths to steady herself. She kept the barrel raised in front of her as she traced her steps back around the house and climbed the stairs to her bedroom. Nothing disturbed the stillness of the shadows except the light breeze billowing the curtains. She entered cautiously, aiming her rifle at the dark corners of the room until she'd ascertained she was alone.

She peered out the open window at the trail of blood on the outside wall, then examined the sill and floorboards. She'd missed them that morning, but now she noticed the stains, hastily wiped down: one partial footprint remained near the bed, and Luisa didn't need to compare to know it matched hers.

Don't let your father see, Luisa's mother had said in her dream.

She understood the warning now. Pa had enough on his mind already; it'd only have worried him even more, but Luisa needed to know. Something stuck out from under the bed; she crouched for a better look, though she already knew what she'd find there.

Her ruined nightgown, rolled up in a ball inside the metal basin. The red dress of her dream, except it wasn't cochineal that gave it its colour. The sponge and towels were tucked underneath, stiff with dried blood.

Luisa dropped the garment. She pressed her hands to her mouth to muffle a scream, then frantically turned them over in a moonbeam: they were mostly clean, but a little blood still stuck to the underside of her broken fingernails, like she'd clawed at something.

The back wall of the house, for instance.

Luisa ran back outside to—where? Where could she even go? There was no escaping herself or what she now knew. Her chest heaved with painful sobs. The plains were a moonlit blur through her tears, and she spun around in panic until she heard the grass calling her name again.

Luisa.

She swiped at her eyes and followed the voice. There, like a beacon in the dark: a woman in a red dress, like a wound drenched in moonlight.

"Mami?" she asked, but no, it couldn't be: she had to be dreaming, she had to have fallen asleep—

"Cariño," the woman—*Mami*—said. "You remember me."

Luisa ran into her mother's arms. "Mami," she cried, breathing her familiar scent: wild thyme and the sharp tang of bruised raspberries, or maybe metal. "I thought you were *dead*. Pa said...Pa said Mr. Wilson killed you. He said he *hated* you."

"Oh, Luisa, my dear girl," she said, holding her tighter. "Mr. Wilson was scared. He did what anyone might have done, seeing what he saw. But I had to find some way to come back."

The fledgling hope in Luisa's heart crumpled again. "Then...you really are gone? This is just another dream, then?"

Mami cupped Luisa's face, smiling adoringly. "There's no such thing as just dreams. Your pa tried his best, but there are things only I can show you."

Luisa sniffled. "Like what?"

"You've been sleepwalking, haven't you?" Luisa's mind raced to keep up, but that was the only explanation; she wiped her tears and nodded. "It's the hungers. You must feed, and I will teach you how. No more killings."

Her mother's cold hand took hers, and as she spoke, she led her toward the sleeping cattle. They neared a bull in the moonlit plain, and Luisa understood. "Then...the heifer? Mr. Wilson? It really was me?"

"You're a good girl, but you must learn to tame your urges, and for that you must first *know* them."

Luisa's eyes welled up again. "I didn't mean to. I swear I didn't mean to hurt anyone, and now the sheriff thinks Pa—"

Mami shushed her gently, then kissed her brow like she was putting her to sleep when Luisa was still a baby. "Later. You must feed first."

So saying, she guided Luisa on top of the bull. It snorted in annoyance, but it knew her; it let her, even as she closed her arms around its neck and her legs around its haunches. Its body heat seeped through her clothes, and its pungent, animal smell filled her nostrils, not unpleasant.

"There you go, cariño," Mami said, stroking her hair. "Now let it out."

Luisa opened her mouth, and gulps of air rushed into her chest. Something rose up her throat, and she tried to snap her lips shut again, but her body refused to obey, like it knew something she didn't. Fresh tears rolled down her face as she tried to resist the nameless urge. It felt...strange, like she was about to throw up, but good. It felt *right*.

It scared her.

"Let it out, Luisa," her mother whispered. "Let it out."

Luisa let it out. A thick, fleshy tendril unfurled from her mouth, questing, and sank into the bull's neck. It bucked, trying to throw her off, but she held on, arms and thighs closed tight around the powerful, rippling muscles.

Blood rolled down her throat and filled her stomach, warming her, sating her at last.

DEAD RECKONING

DEBORAH TAPPER

SAM "SILVER" Yancey wouldn't stay dead.

First time he died, Marshal Nate Wing shot him on a Tuesday afternoon. He bled out in the red dust just opposite Lou's, with the ladies crowding the windows and a whole bunch of us standing around. No one shed any tears; we were all too glad to see him go.

He didn't go easy, mind. Coughing, spitting, air wheezing in and out of that hole the marshal's Peacemaker had punched through his ribs. You could practically hear his lungs filling with blood as he drowned right there in the dry August heat. He didn't say much, either. Just cursed us all before he went.

Typical Silver.

Six of us buried him up at Boot Hill an hour later, where he'd be in good company. Doc Philips took his picture first with his new-fangled camera, before the undertaker nailed the lid down on his coffin. Silver had his eyes closed, but afterward Doc swore he'd opened them for an instant and winked. Course he wasn't winking when Doc processed the plate and framed the picture, although everyone said he looked kind of cheery for a dead man, like he knew something we didn't.

Anyway, we were up at Boot Hill, digging the hole. It was a killer hot day and I guess we were all privately thinking this was far too much trouble for someone like Silver, who'd never done a single good thing for anyone in all his thirty years. Clayton Perry even went so far as to suggest we should just tip him out the coffin and leave him where he lay for the vultures and coyotes to find, but that seemed a little too harsh, even for Silver.

Clayton Perry was the first to die.

You'd have expected it to be Marshal Wing, seeing as he's the one who put that initial bullet through Silver. But no, it was Clayton we found dead, with the skin pulled clean off his bones. And not in his own bed, either; he was over at Lou's with Irish Molly, one of her best girls. Molly was incoherent with terror and it took a while for Marshal Wing to coax the story from her. Seems she'd fallen asleep—something she normally never did when entertaining a gentleman—then woken to find Clayton lying next to her, in a state of more complete undress than she'd ever seen before.

Doc Philips lugged his camera over to Lou's and photographed Clayton—more for curiosity's sake than anything—then pronounced him dead, most likely murdered.

Seemed like a shrewd assumption.

We were all too astonished by Clayton's murder to wonder where his skin had gone, until the undertaker arrived to stow him in a coffin and noticed it was missing.

Whoever killed him had taken it with them.

Not long after that, another of Lou's girls claimed she'd seen Silver Yancey peeking in at her through a window with his eyes gone and his tongue lolling over his jaw. No one paid too much attention to the story: Lou's girls were the finest in town, and people were always trying to peek in without paying. Lou bought another shotgun just in case and hired herself some protection in the shape of the Flynn Brothers.

And Billy Flynn was the second person to shoot Silver dead.

Silver didn't look half so handsome as he'd done the first time he died, what with his rotted eyes and his skin gone all shiny green-gray and stinking like you wouldn't believe. Young Billy Flynn put six rounds in him—five more than Marshal Wing had—and even then it seemed Silver wasn't ready to give up. He kept crawling and bubbling until Billy's two big brothers beat him to...death?

Beat him until he stopped moving, anyway.

Doc Philips examined the body and decided Silver couldn't have been properly dead when we buried him, despite the fact he certainly looked like he'd been gone for three weeks. But he was dead now, no doubt about it.

He paid the Flynn brothers a dollar each to hold the body up for another photograph—with young Billy posing beside it, revolver in his hand.

There didn't seem to be any point putting him in a new coffin, so the same little group of us who'd shovelled the soil in over him on that sweltering Tuesday afternoon—minus poor Clayton Perry, obviously—trekked back up to Boot Hill intending to dig it up again.

Soon as we got there, we realized Silver had saved us the trouble.

The grave was busted open, the rocks we'd dumped on top scattered. Everyone swore it wasn't the work of a normal man. And since I was the fastest runner, they sent me back for the preacher, who came puffing after me and said some strong prayers over the grave before we pulled Silver's coffin back out. The lid was splintered into tiny fragments, but we figured it'd be easy enough for the undertaker to nail a new one in place.

Once Silver was safely back inside, we buried him for the second time.

We collected a ton of rocks, piling them over the grave until we were sure nothing could get out—not even a man as desperate and determined as Sam "Silver" Yancey.

Then we went back and hit the saloon, aiming to get as drunk as it took to forget that grin we'd all seen on Silver's eyeless face just before the lid went on.

The two eldest Flynn brothers died a few days later, torn apart and strewn around just like those rocks we'd put over Silver's grave. After young Billy had found what he could of his brothers, Marshal Wing called for help in locating all the other missing parts.

And I was one of those fool enough to volunteer.

Guess I should've drunk a few more bottles of whiskey after we buried Silver.

We searched the town, but the scavengers hadn't left much to find—and the few bits we did find had no bones in them.

Clayton Perry had lost his skin.

And now it seemed someone had taken the Flynn brothers' bones.

We all knew who that "someone" was.

Billy took his brothers' deaths real hard, emptying endless bottles of whiskey and swearing vengeance on a dead man. The day after we buried his brothers, he disappeared. People said he'd upped and left town, but I had a sneaking suspicion that old Silver hadn't quite finished with the Flynn brothers.

And I was right.

Billy's things were still in the room he'd shared with his brothers —and so was he, folded up neatly and crammed in a closet.

He'd set solid in there, so Marshal Wing and Doc Philips wrestled him out between them. And when the Doc examined him, he noticed Billy's chest was all smashed open and someone had ripped his lungs out, most likely while he was still using them to breathe.

Something had to be done.

So I talked to the other guys who'd buried Silver. And after fortifying ourselves with a drink or four, we went up to Boot Hill to put an end to this thing once and for all.

It was September, just over a month since Marshal Wing first shot Silver dead outside Lou's—and already four honest people were gone. We already knew what we were going to find when we got there. Even so, we five stood around Silver's opened grave with our picks and shovels, staring down at the empty coffin as if we could stare Silver back into it.

"He's out," I said, stating the obvious as usual.

The others just looked at me with bewildered eyes. "So what do we do, Lucky?" Pete Chu asked. "Keep killing him until he gets the message and stays put?"

I shrugged and leaned on my shovel, wondering why I was supposed to have all the answers. "Guess it's all we can do," I said, thinking of Billy Flynn's missing lungs and the way the breath wheezed out through that hole in Silver's chest.

Ben Tyler nodded, but Luis Garcia and Virgil Pickering weren't so sure. "Killing him means finding him," Virgil said. "And if he ain't here, where is he?"

"In town," I said. "Somewhere. Looking for his next victim."

Luis glanced around at the other Boot Hill graves, with their undisturbed stones and inactive occupants. "Who's he gonna pick, Lucky?"

He picked Luis.

Then Virgil.

Then Ben.

And finally Pete Chu.

Taking their muscles and tendons, their flesh and blood.

Guess it was my turn next.

If I'd had even so much as a pinch of sense, I'd have hightailed it soon as I found Luis all ripped up like that. But I'm the stubborn sort, and I wasn't going to be chased out of town by a small-time crook I'd buried twice already.

So I stayed.

And I vowed I'd be the one to take Silver Yancey out for good this time.

Even so, I couldn't keep my eyes open constantly, so I hired a guy to watch my back while I slept. There was some wild gossip going around town thanks to Lou's girls, but most people didn't know the truth about Silver. All they knew was that eight people had died in unpleasant ways recently. I didn't mention I was square in Silver's sights, either; I just said this was all to do with an unfortunate misunderstanding involving a game of cards.

Since I turn a tidy profit in the gambling halls and saloons, he believed me.

Another pair of eyes was good, but I went to the gunsmiths for some extra firepower just in case. And then I bought the biggest axe I could find.

Silver thought he'd tuck me up in the ground.

But in reality, I was going to put Silver back where he belonged.

All I had to do was wait.

I was so sure Silver was coming for me. I mean, he'd picked off every other man in the burying party; seemed beyond reason he'd pass over me. But that's exactly what he did do. Because the next death wasn't yours truly, Lucky Henry Haines.

It was Doc Philips.

Marshal Wing found him, propped up in front of his camera with an exposed glass plate and an empty head. Seemed Silver had cut the top off Doc's skull with one of his own saws and scooped out his brains.

Marshal Wing asked around and found someone who knew how to develop the plate. I was there when the photograph was printed, and it showed Silver grinning and pinning Doc down as he sawed his way through flesh and bone.

Doc was still alive when he started cutting.

I really thought it was my turn after Doc died. But Silver killed Marshal Wing instead, using a pair of Doc's bone shears to chop through his ribs and take his heart.

After that, it could only be me next.

I hired a second bodyguard. Shut myself away with my guns and big axe, waiting for Silver to make his move. Only slept for ten minutes at a time. Silver wasn't going to surprise me like he'd surprised Doc and Marshal Wing.

But he surprised both my bodyguards.

I was catnapping when something disturbed me. The faint

drumming of boot heels on the floor, maybe. Or the hint of a groan. Either way, I was on my feet with the axe clenched in both hands almost before my eyes had opened.

Silver was standing a few paces away, grinning at me.

The stink of him rolled over me, making my eyes water and my stomach heave. "You look ready to fall apart, Silver," I said, trying not to breathe too deeply.

"Guess I am." Silver didn't seem too bothered by his imminent dissolution. "And you, Henry Haines—think you're still *lucky*?"

I gripped the axe tighter. "Come a little closer and find out."

"Maybe I will." Gloopy black slime drooled over Silver's chin, dribbling down onto a shirtfront already crusted with putrescence. "You've sure got some guts or you would've run by now, Lucky. Guts, and no brains. But that's okay—guts are what I need."

He leapt at me, bony fingers hooked like claws.

And I swung the axe.

The first swing hacked a hole in his chest, smashing through his ribs. He snarled and I wrenched the axe free. Swung again, chopping his right arm off this time. Another swing sent his head rolling across the floor and under my bed.

I kept chopping and chopping.

I swung that axe until all that was left of Sam "Silver" Yancey was a heap of stinking meat and offal.

The two men I'd hired were dead, too. Silver had ripped them up and had their eyes—which is ironic, since they never saw him coming. But I couldn't worry about them; I needed to get Silver back to Boot Hill and safely in his grave.

I'd got a sack ready and waiting, so I gathered up every piece—crawling under the bed first to retrieve his head—and dumped old Silver inside, bit by reeking bit. Once I was sure I'd got everything, I heaved the sack over my shoulder and set off.

I was sweating by the time I got there, but Silver was in the sack and I'd survived. I walked up to his open grave and dumped the sack straight in the empty coffin. "You're dead, Silver," I said. "So you just accept it and stay put this time."

The sack said nothing.

I went back to the town. Got a new coffin lid. Hammer and nails. A shovel. Walked back up, intending to do this properly and nail the lid down over Silver.

The sack was empty.

Something smashed into me as I started to pull my gun, knocking it out of my hand and slamming me face down on the stony ground. I tried to fight, but Silver was back in one piece and far stronger than I could've ever imagined. And he was dead, so my punches had no effect.

I kept fighting, even when I knew it was hopeless and I was going to die as surely as all the others had. I pummelled and tore at rotting flesh. Dug my fingers into sludgy sockets. Ripped half his face away, exposing the festering bones.

Silver just laughed.

"No brains," he said. "But guts, Lucky—you've got *guts*!"

His finger bones felt like ten knives as they sliced into my flesh, opening my belly.

I yelled. Fought harder than I've ever fought before. But Silver only chuckled and plunged his filthy clawed hands deeper into my guts, beginning to pull them out.

It *hurt*.

Hurt like you wouldn't believe.

I yelled and fought and at some point I started screaming. Silver took no notice. He just laughed and pulled—pulled and laughed—and when the pulling and laughing finally stopped, my guts were piled beside me, all shivery and glistening.

I was shivering, too. "Silver..." I croaked, wondering how I could still be alive and talking with my guts on the ground like this.

"You ratted me off to Marshal Wing," Silver said. "That's why I saved you for last."

"How?" Sweat popped across my forehead, trickling into my eyes. "Why won't you stay dead?"

"Because I made the deal of my *life*." He grinned with what remained of his face. "Now who's lucky?"

"What deal?" I said, although I could guess.

"One you'd never believe." Silver scratched his decaying chin. "That's why I'm still standing—and you're not. And why you'll never get to leave."

He grabbed me by the ankles and dragged me over to his grave. Rolled me in with a casual kick. "Here lies Lucky Henry Haines," he said, grinning down. "Short on guts—and shorter on brains."

I could hear him laughing as he walked away.

I lay in the coffin, wishing I could stop so the pain would stop, too. But I didn't stop. And neither did the pain.

After what seemed like forever, a shadow fell over the grave. I squinted up and saw Clayton Perry smiling down at me.

"Clay...?" I whispered.

"His face looks good on me, don't it?" Silver ran a hand along Clayton's jaw, settling it more securely over a Flynn brother's skull. He looked new, healthy—*alive*. "Just came past to say goodbye. And to get rid of this, seeing as I don't need it no more."

His old body slithered into the grave on top of me, slimy and stinking. Then he picked up the coffin lid I'd brought for him and nailed it in place.

I lay in darkness, listening as he shovelled the soil back over me.

I guess I must've died at some point. My body held me in place for a very long time, but as it turned to mush and bone I gradually felt the ties getting lighter and lighter—until at last I could kick free of it and escape.

I dug my way up through the coffin lid. Through soil and rock. Kept digging until my hands and head broke the surface and I could feel the fresh air on my skin.

Silver was long gone. I turned my back on the grave and started walking. But I'd only gone twenty paces when a snapping jerk stopped me in my tracks, like I'd reached the end of a short rope. I tried walking in other directions—then every direction—but I couldn't get any farther than twenty paces away from my grave.

Then I remembered what Silver said.

About how I'd never leave.

I climb back down to my grave sometimes. Sleep for a decade or so. But usually I'm up top as I call it, sitting here on the piled stones by my grave marker. Silver must've put it up before he left, complete with its insulting little epitaph.

A long time's passed away since I did, and the old town's famous now. People come here to tend the graves or take pictures of themselves by the markers, although not with glass plate cameras like Doc Philips used.

They never see me, just like *you* can't see me. Can't hear me, either. All the same, I like to talk to them sometimes, explain how I came to be buried here and why I can't leave. I talk and they don't hear. They just laugh at my epitaph and Lucky Henry Haines, a man short of both guts *and* brains.

Fool I may be. But I never lacked courage—which is why I'll still be sitting here when this heap of rocks has crumbled to dust and Boot Hill with it.

All the same, being dead's given me plenty of time to think. Mostly about Silver—and that deal of his. And about how maybe *I* could make a deal, too. The kind nobody should make, unless they're just too hungry for revenge to care about the consequences.

Silver's confident that he and I are done.

But I'm not so sure.

A FIST FULL OF DIRT

E.M. OTERO

CARLOS CLEANED the blood from his tomahawk and scowled at the filth of the other men as they pried into the crates on the wagon. Dusty's runny nose cut rivers in the dust of his face, and the snot crusted on his sleeves from his constant wiping.

The heist had gone flawlessly—other than the shooting and killing—but all seven of their gang came out uninjured.

"It's not heavy enough to be filled with gold, but maybe jewelry, or even cash," Boone said excitedly. All Carlos knew was that Boone, their gang leader, said that some guy paid a lot of money to ship these crates and all the people on the train to New York.

Carlos shivered, remembering the folks on the train. Their vacant, sunken eyes, the way their lower jaws receded, making their necks long and birdlike. Then there was the smell, like turned earth and rotten flesh.

Still worse was the way the passengers came after them when they stole the crates. Like a pack of feral animals. Carlos couldn't shake the image of the last man he shot, from the back of his horse. The man's skull exploded, but he kept running like nothing happened. Carlos watched half the man's head fall to the ground, and as that man ran with the sun at his back, Carlos swore he saw—

The first box's lid came off, the sound of the wood snapping thrusting Carlos into the present. A musty smell, like the odor under a wet log, filled the air. Boone stared dumbstruck at its contents. Carlos didn't move at first; this wouldn't be the first heist where what they stole wasn't worth piss.

Dusty dug his hands in and pulled out clumps of wet soil. "It's jus' dirt."

"No, it can't be," Boone said, digging through the earth. "No, no, no! There has to be something buried here. It can't be just dirt!"

He yanked the box off the wagon, dumping the contents onto the ground, revealing it was just soil.

Dusty rubbed his face, smearing the dark soil across his nose and mouth. "Well, shit."

"Check the others!" Boone shouted, and the large brutish man called Brock smashed the last five boxes open. Just like the first, there was only soil.

Boone kicked the dirt, sending bits of it into the air and splattering it over their camp. A large clump landed in front of Carlos as he finished cleaning the tomahawk and started on his Winchester. His eyes fixed on the wet dark lump, and his hands and arms itched from the feeling of phantom dirt on his skin. He resisted the urge to stop and clean himself and cursed under his breath. Watching another person become soiled was enough to feel the taint on his own flesh.

Everyone stayed quiet, knowing it was best to leave Boone to his tantrums, since he had a way of taking out his frustration on anyone or thing within reach.

"Dammit all to hell!" he said through gritted teeth as he wiped down his arms with a rag. Then Boone threw the rag in Brock's face, smearing him with dirt, before stomping into the woods.

"At least he didn't overreact," Francis said, admiring the inside of his hat. Brock chuckled, and Carlos nodded, noting the sarcasm. He still couldn't take his eyes off the clump of soil, though. It was more than his compulsion to stay clean; the dirt was wrong. It could have been a trick of the dancing flame, but as Carlos stared, it seemed to move. The dark clump writhed, and small sorrel shapes uncoiled into segmented, elongated creatures.

Worms.

They spread from the clump, seeming to test the surrounding ground before disappearing from sight. It was unnerving, and Carlos couldn't rationalize why. It was dirt, and dirt had worms, but watching them penetrate the loam left him feeling unclean.

Carlos stood, found some water and washed himself till his skin was red and imagined taint was clean.

That night, rest eluded Carlos. He kept having dreams that the ground under his bedroll was writhing with worms. Their squirming russet bodies moved the soil, so it undulated like water and pushed him toward the dark woods where something was waiting. He couldn't escape, his arms and feet bound by mounds of wriggling bodies, and as he got close to the trees, a man stepped from the dark.

He wore half a bloody smile on half a face, the rest blown apart by the bullet Carlos put through his head. In that void where the rest of the man's skull should have been was—

A branch snapping pulled Carlos from the dream, and the stillness of the ground was disorienting at first. Adjusting to wakefulness, he listened without moving or fully opening his eyes, trying to place the sound. Francis was supposed to be on watch, and he knew better than to wander off without waking someone else. It came again a moment later—the disturbance of the forest floor by a clumsy shoe. Either someone was extremely bad at being stealthy, or they didn't care. The first image in his mind was of the man with half a head finally catching up after stumbling after them all night.

Carlos opened his eyes and checked his surroundings. The fire was only cinders, and as he searched, he noticed Francis was asleep but Brock wasn't in his bed roll or sitting near the fire. Then he saw the large man, standing at the edge of their camp staring into the darkness. Carlos rose, keeping his tomahawks close. The man was completely still, and didn't move when Carlos called out his name.

He touched his shoulder and whispered. "Brock, do you see something?"

Brock jumped at the sound and looked confused. "I...uh," he stammered. "I don't remember getting up."

Carlos nodded. "Lay back down; we can't have you sleepwalking off into the woods now."

Brock looked back out and said, "No, can't have that."

Brock had never sleepwalked in all the time Carlos had been part of the gang. It was strange, but not enough to worry about. Soon, Carlos drifted back off to a restless sleep.

In the morning, Boone opted to head to the next town. His mood had leveled back out, but there was still a tension that was as thick as a horsehide.

As the morning crawled by, Carlos noticed Brock talking to his hand. It reminded him of children playing pretend, but something about it made his palms itch.

Carlos, Francis, Dusty, and Boone traded looks whenever Brock giggled loudly while looking at his palm. Carlos rode his horse, Viento, next to Brock, and as Carlos got closer, he noticed something strange on the big man's hand. Before he could get a good look, Brock closed his palm and turned toward Carlos.

"What do you want?" Brock asked.

"Wanted to make sure you were alright," Carlos stated, his eyes still on the man's closed fist.

"I'm fine," Brock said and moved his horse forward, putting distance between them.

Carlos shook his head, trying to rationalize what he'd seen in Brock's hand. He wasn't certain, and as he tried to recall the image, it made him feel queasy. It made him think of the man with half a head too. Those images, while different, were both grotesque, because Brock's hand looked like the skin had wrinkled and contorted to form a face.

As they rode, Dusty picked at his skin more than usual. In the past, Carlos had observed Dusty digging his dirty nails across his arm, peeling off a scab and, after careful inspection, eating it. As grotesque as Carlos found that, this was far worse. Dusty dug into virgin skin, muttering about something being under there. Carlos fought the urge to clean his hands every time he noticed the man's excoriation, and eventually ignored him all together.

Then, halfway through the day, Brock picked up a few branches and started whittling. Not once had Carlos ever seen the man do anything like it. As he carved, he nodded, and gave affirmative noises as the unusual object he created took shape. Instead of creating a likeness of something, he peeled away the bark, and along one side he made dozens of notches.

The strangeness of the last day was getting on Carlos's nerves, and he could tell it was affecting the others too. The heist, the crates of soil, and now the peculiar behavior. It was enough to drive anyone mad. It didn't help that in every shadow he swore he saw the man with half a head, and what coiled and writhed from the ravaged skull.

The image of that man was burned into his mind, the blood-red sky silhouetting his shape, as gore erupted from his shattered head, and then what came after. The shadowy worm-like tendrils had tasted the air like worms searching for dirt to burrow in.

The strangeness came to a climax in the evening. While they were making camp, Dusty took his skinning knife to his arm.

"They're under my skin!" he shrieked, digging the blade into his forearm before pulling at a tendon with the tip of the knife. Everyone stood frozen for a moment before lunging at him, pulling the knife from his hands.

"They're under my skin! I need to get them out! Please help me!" Dusty cried out repeatedly. Carlos, Francis, and Boone tied him up, bandaged his wound, unsure of what to do. After a while of shrieking and trying to gnaw at his arms and wrists, they gagged him as well.

"He has lost it, madder than a hatter," Francis drawled, shaking his head. "He cut that tendon. I think he went and ruined that hand."

"We need to get him to a doctor," Boone said, pushing a stick into the fire, releasing a bout of sparks.

"What does he think is under his skin?" Carlos asked, ignoring the itch of his palms.

"It's the worms," Brock said in a cheerful tone. Every face turned to him as he gazed into the warm glow. He sat farther back than everyone else, the fire illuminating only his hands and face. "I can hear them."

"What the fuck are you talking about?" Boone asked, then spat on the ground.

"The worms. They're having trouble with Dusty. Unlike me."

Carlos remembered the clump of dirt that a large segmented worm uncoiled from, and wondered if Dusty somehow got one of those worms inside him. Perhaps it had eggs or something in the dirt, and when he rubbed his nose, they—no, that would be too far-fetched. His palms itched, more phantom soil needing to be cleansed.

"Explain," Carlos said, cutting the confused silence.

"Dusty is rejecting them, fighting his gift. He should just listen to the worms." Brock smiled, his teeth reflecting the flames, giving him a bloody grin.

"You lost it, and I am too tired to listen to this shit anymore," Boone said and returned to his roll in the wagon and announced,

"We should take shifts being on watch, at least for a few more nights."

Carlos volunteered to take the first watch, and everyone curled up to sleep. His eyes didn't wander far from Brock as he continued to whisper to his hand. If there was going to be any danger tonight, he was certain that man mumbling about worms would be its source.

It didn't take long for everyone's breaths to slow to the rhythmic melody of sleep, but Carlos was certain Brock wasn't sleeping. Rather than his usual child-like rolling about, and eventual twitchy fitful sleep on his side, Brock was on his back staring straight up at the stars.

Carlos noted some movement on the ground between his booted feet. The sand whirled and shifted like when a strong wind blows. Only the air was still. He kept his eye on it, and for a moment the shifting topography of the dirt made a face of grooves and lines. Carlos, startled, kicked the dirt, breaking the strange hallucination apart.

An hour later when Brock said he would take over watch, Carlos put a few extra logs on the fire to keep it burning bright, and lay down in his roll. Instead of going to sleep, he watched the strange man, hoping his assumptions weren't true. If Brock had gone mad, he would have to put him down. His hands itched at the thought, but not as intensely as when he felt the phantom dirt. The imagined blood from his anticipation was always an easier compulsion to ease than dirt.

Carlos lay still, and mimicked the slow breaths of sleep, while watching. Brock whispered, but no one else was awake. Carlos imagined Brock talking to the man with half a head, and strained to look into the woods to see if there was a person there to talk to.

There was only darkness.

Then, Brock pulled out the wood he had whittled earlier, and another stick. He pushed the serrated stick into the ground and rubbed the other one up and down the bumps, creating a dull wooden clatter.

The sound wasn't loud, but it made Carlos uncomfortable. He sat up on his roll, one of his tomahawks already gripped in his hand. Nothing happened, though he continued the clatter for a long time. Carlos wondered if this strange instrument had a purpose other than keeping him awake. It certainly was working.

Then his eye caught movement along the ground. Shifting and writhing in the sand and dirt were worms. First, he noticed only a couple, but the numbers increased and soon the entire ground was shifting and squirming, just like in his dream.

Brock giggled. "Here is your offering, my Prince."

Carlos stood up and shouted, "What the hell is this, Brock?"

He turned toward Carlos, his eyes bright and smile wide. In the firelight he could see that Brock's veins moved under his skin, like worms in the ground below. "Why, Carlos, this is a tithe, an induction into greatness. The Prince Beneath needs more vessels."

"The prince? What are you raving about?" The worms were crawling over his roll now, trying to find a way into his boots. Carlos paced to prevent them from gaining purchase.

Brock stood, gesturing to the others. "They are going to join his kingdom. Don't you understand? The Prince and his acolytes are a tribe of lovers. They love us and want us to be one with them."

Carlos looked at Francis and Dusty; worms squirmed over them. They were writhing into their ears, nose and even their eyes as they slept.

"Boone, wake up!" Carlos shouted, but he didn't respond. Worms wrapped around the spokes of the wagon wheel, trying climbing to their other offering.

"They can't hear you," Brock said in a singsong voice. "They are ascending, like you soon will." Brock stepped closer with his arms spread wide, and as he moved between the fire and Carlos, his shadow extended out toward him. "Look, you can see for yourself."

Brock presented his hand, and in his palm was a face made from the contorted flesh. Carlos felt his hands and arms itch while his gut twisted in revulsion. Then the face shifted and moved, like something was crawling under the man's skin.

Carlos made a quick decision. With the swift, liquid motion of a well-practiced act, the tomahawk left his hand. The blade struck Brock's skull with a wet *thunk*.

"I'm sorry, Brock, you were a good—" Carlos stopped. As he watched, Brock reached up, grabbed the handle of his tomahawk and pulled it free. The wound wept dark blood for only a second. Black spidery tendrils reached to each other from across the wound and pulled it shut.

"He changed me, Carlos." His smile grew wider. "The Prince of Worms is a lover of man, and he grants gifts to those he loves."

Without hesitating, Carlos threw his second tomahawk. This one Brock plucked from the air as if a child had thrown it. What he wasn't ready for was Carlos charging him, ramming his shoulder into the thing he once knew as Brock, knocking him onto the fire.

Brock's clothes caught fire immediately, and his scream was brief and more confused than pained. Dusty sat up, and with a vacant stare, watched the man flail and burn. Carlos grabbed the two tomahawks, thankful that Brock had dropped them before his tumble.

Dusty, still sitting with his hands and legs bound, turned his head to Carlos. "I can hear them. I can hear *him*." His skin rippled like snakes on water. "We shouldn't be afraid, Carlos. We give sight to the blind." Dusty snapped his bindings like they were made of paper.

"They are lovers of man." An exultant voice that was not his came from Francis's mouth. "If it weren't for us, they wouldn't know the world above."

Francis stood, raising his revolver toward Carlos and said, "The dark will be our light, and if you can't accept these gifts, then—" The crack of a gunshot cut the soft voices, and half of Francis's head exploded, but he didn't fall. Instead, he turned to look at the source of the gunshot.

Boone knelt in the wagon, his repeater trained on Dusty. "Don't move, or I will put a hole in every single one of you."

"You underestimate us," Dusty said with an inhuman sneer. Francis raised his revolver, even as gore drained from the crater in his skull. Carlos tossed his tomahawk, the blade sinking in Francis's arm, sending his shot wide. Boone fired at Dusty in three quick bursts, putting massive holes in his chest. Carlos slammed his other tomahawk into the remains of Francis' face, and as he collapsed Carlos had to kick the falling man in the chest to free his weapon.

Boone fired on them both as Carlos whistled for Viento and found his Winchester by his bedroll.

"I think that's everyone!" Boone shouted as he hopped off the wagon.

Carlos whistled again, and Viento came from the dark, but the horse nickered a short distance away, refusing to come closer.

Carlos grabbed a cloth to wipe his tomahawk's blade and noticed something moving in the blood. Black, hair-thin worms were wriggling like a fish in a crimson ocean.

"What the fuck happened to them?" Boone asked as he loaded his rifle.

There was the sound of something dragging, and an inhuman voice said, "The Prince of Worms blessed them; they became vessels."

Boone looked for the source, and Brock looked up at him, his body charred black. "Don't be afraid, Boone. The Prince is a deity of love." His skin cracked and flaked as he spoke.

Boone placed his rifle on Brock's forehead. "I don't need any love from a damn prince." He pulled the trigger, and Brock's head disappeared in a red mist.

"We need you though," a voice said from a few feet away. Carlos and Boone turned to see Francis's body being stitched together by writhing wormlike tendrils stretching between the wounds and gore. "We can't live without you. You give sight to the blind, and we give you the gift of our love to show gratitude."

Francis's body not only repaired itself, but pulled in the other bodies near it. Carlos and Boone watched in abject terror as the flesh of their gang was molded like clay by invisible hands.

Multiple voices spoke from the same amalgam of bodies.

"You can complete us."

"The dark is our light."

"Aren't you tired of being alone?"

"Can't you hear that? That sound of the worms in song."

"We are a species, a tribe of lovers, and we love—"

Boone started shooting, and the bullets, while striking the mass of bodies, sending gouts of blood into the air, seemed to have no effect.

"That's no way to show gratitude," the voices said in unison and with the speed of a snake strike, a hand made of fingers and limbs stretched horribly long, snatched Boone. His bones cracked and snapped in the monster's grip.

"We will remake you, bone, flesh, and all."

Carlos grabbed a bottle of Dusty's liquor and threw it at the fire, breaking the glass. The eruption of flame caused the monster to scream in a cacophony of voices, like a house burning down with people inside. The flames gave Carlos enough time to run to Viento, mount him and take off. A roar unlike anything on earth shattered the peace of the night, as flames caught on the wagon and nearby brush. It looked and sounded as if the gates of hell had opened.

Carlos rode till dawn, and as the sun rose, he felt it was time to rest. Finding a stream to clean himself and his clothes, he felt the weariness take hold and collapsed on the ground and stared at the trickling water, pondering the events of the night.

He took off his gloves to clean his hands in the fresh water of the stream. He scrubbed them clean, scouring away the dirt, blood, shame, and the fear. Once his hands were red and raw, he walked back to his horse.

Then something moving in the damp earth next to the stream caught his eye.

Lines formed as if made by an invisible finger. The lines shifted and changed until they sculpted a face.

Its mouth moved, and a sound like rocks grinding became words. "We are a species of lovers. Join us and spread our love."

Worms emerged from the damp earth. Carlos kicked it, distorting the face and sending the worms into the stream. The voice kept talking anyway. "Give sight to those below, and the darkness will be our light."

"Shut the fuck up," he said through gritted teeth.

"The Prince of Worms, Desolation himself, has your scent; he knows the sound and cadence of your gait. We are a patient species, especially him, and he loves fighters like you."

"Patient." Carlos chuckled. "There are two types of men in the world, those who end up in the dirt, and those who put them there."

The horrible voice cackled from another face formed in the dirt a few feet away. "We are spreading, his influence grows and we will—"

Carlos kicked that one too, mounted Viento and rode off, keeping his eyes above the ground. He knew it was only a matter of time before they caught up, and he would hear that voice again. *We are a species of lovers, Carlos...*

They could chase him, track him from heaven to hell, but if they truly knew his scent, they would only find it on the bodies of their vessels. Even if they ended up beneath his feet hiding, waiting for him to make a mistake, Carlos wasn't going to let the worms win.

He wasn't the type of man to end up in the dirt.

DESMODUS

SCOTTY MILDER

THE WEATHER WAS COLD, but hadn't yet turned surly.

Daddy was trying to fix up the porch railing. Garfield, their old Missouri Fox Trotter, had chewed on it all spring and summer and now the termites had got all in there. Daddy wanted to get the work done before the snows came.

He set up two crooked sawhorses above the slope that rolled down to the Animas Forks Road, ran a length of pine across them, and got to cutting. Dottie Mae sat up on the porch, mending a pair of trousers, now and then looking up to watch him work.

The job went smooth at first. But then the brand-new saw he'd picked up in anticipation of the task began stripping its teeth.

Daddy growled and tossed the useless blade aside. It clattered across the gravel. Sparky, their old sheepdog mutt, wandered over to sniff it.

"You thirsty, Daddy?" Dottie asked, trying to distract him. "You want I should go fetch some water, and maybe a bear sign off'n the stove to go 'long with it?"

Daddy wiped his brow. It was getting chilly—the mountain air starting to sprout winter teeth—but he was still sweating through his burlaps.

"Naw. What I'd like is for you to go fetch my old bow saw from out the shed," he said. "It's rusted over, but it ought to help me buckle to."

"Okay." She set the trousers aside and brushed at her dress and coat, preemptively concerned about the dust. It was always swirling around in the shed, making the air taste like dry old death.

"It's hanging from a peg by the door," Dad called after her as she made her way up the path toward where the shed and outhouse knuckled sharply out of a sandstone bluff. "And if'n you see any critters, you just leave 'em be. Rex Montoya down the livery said there's been a bout of canine madness going around."

"Alright, Daddy!" Dottie Mae called back, and went skipping the rest of the way.

The shed door opened with a scream. Daylight shrank back, startled. Hot darkness rolled out and, as expected, its breath was pungent with corruption. It wasn't as bad as the outhouse, but at least with the outhouse she could put her finger on what was foul. Piss and shit would never smell like roses, Daddy said, no matter how deep you buried it.

This was different. The blistering odor was noxious but unknowable. It made Dottie Mae think of old logs teeming with beetles, rocks melting under a blazing sun, charred bones, the empty blackness between the stars. Dottie Mae wasn't afraid of the shed, exactly, but she didn't much like it neither. This dry, barren smell would linger in her nostrils for the rest of the day, and leave her unsettled.

She let her eyes adjust. Slowly, the contours of the space came into focus. The walls were rough pine planks, hammered so close together that only the thinnest razors of sunlight pushed through the gaps. An old table sat to the left of the door, piled high with crates. A Winchester rifle—rusted clean through its barrel—leaned against it.

Tools—hammers of various sizes, a crudely smithed axe, an even cruder pickaxe—hung from pegs.

And, of course, there was Daddy's old Arkansas Toothpick hanging on a rawhide strap. Its cherry handle was worn smooth, and its blade glinted in the muddy light. Daddy wouldn't have made it all the way from Tennessee to Colorado without that knife, he said. She'd asked him why not. He and Mama exchanged a look. Mama shook her head. Daddy's mouth twisted into a smile, and he tweaked her nose and said *never you mind, Sweetness. Them ain't daisy stories for daisy little girls.*

Two broken wagon wheels rested against a massive oak bureau in the middle of the shed. Other pieces of discarded furniture were lashed to the bureau with heavy ropes.

The bow saw—a crescent of handled walnut joined at each curved end by a rusted band of toothed steel—hung between the pickaxe and the blade. She hurried across the dirt floor and reached for it.

Something skittered in the darkness behind the bureau.

Dottie Mae stopped, her hand hovering inches from the saw. A trickle of ice spurted between her shoulders and into the base of her skull.

Another skitter. Clawed feet scratched against wood.

A squeak.

It's a mouse, dummy. Forget all about it and—

That thought was interrupted by a leathery flapping sound.

She gazed into the silky darkness behind the bureau. *That ain't no mouse.*

Slowly—cursing herself for a fool and yet beset by a pleasant thrum of anticipation—Dottie Mae stepped away from the wall and slithered around the mound of furniture. Too late, it occurred to her that she should have grabbed the toothpick off the wall. The black groped at her with inky tendrils. The smell back here was far, far worse. It went from dry death to a feverish, boiling molder. Dottie Mae had once come across a coyote disemboweled by a rancher's rifle shot, rotting into the summer grass. This smell was like that—except closed in it felt alive, like something wet and smooth worming up her nose and down her throat. She coughed, telling herself not to be sick.

It took Dottie's eyes another ten seconds to identify the furry thing wriggling against the wall.

A bat.

Don't get too close. She thought about the canine madness. Daddy said some folks thought the madness came from bats. She smoothed out her skirt and knelt, feet away, watching it.

It didn't look much like the bats she'd seen flitting in the firelight on Greene Street and between the boulders jutting toothily along the flank of Tower Mountain. Those bats were small like mice, and their fur was the same reddish brown as Mama's hair. This was at least as big as a squirrel, and in the shed's darkness its fur was oily black. One of its wings splayed out across the floor, and it looked eight inches long at least.

Black eyes rolled toward her. The nose had an odd, flayed-open look, fleshy and twitching. Even in the gloom she could see two white teeth jutting from its upper jaw.

It squeaked. In that sharp sound she heard pain, misery, and buzzing animal terror. Her own fear melted away.

"Where'd you come from?" Dottie Mae asked. She wanted to go to the thing and cradle it, stroke its bristly black fur and tell it that everything would be okay. But her Daddy hadn't raised a fool, and she knew what the canine madness could do.

It squeaked again and tried to push itself up with its extended wing. She saw that the other wing hung, bent, off its shoulder.

"You hurt? You get trapped in here and break yourself?"

Another squeak. It seemed that this was of dismayed assent.

"I'll cotton a bet that you're pretty hungry," she said. What did bats eat, exactly? She thought the little red ones she saw in town went after insects. "Hold on," she said.

Once she was outside—gulping at the piney mountain air—she knelt and levered over one of the smooth stones Daddy had set along the path. The soil beneath was black and moist, and even this late in the season it teemed with critters. Brown-carapaced beetles pushed stupidly through the muck. Worms wriggled.

Something scrabbled across rocks nearby. She looked up and saw the old black tomcat up on the rocky ridge above the shed. The cat gazed at her with impassive golden eyes. Beyond it, she could just see the cracked top of a tombstone. That was the old bootyard: a dozen or so overgrown graves, the names on the headstones and bent wooden crosses faded almost to nothing. The bootyard was there long before Daddy came along to build the cabin.

The cat didn't have a name, and Daddy said it had been skulking around before she was born. *How it stays clear of the coyotes, I'll never know.*

"Scat!" Dottie Mae hissed. The tomcat was a mangy thing and she'd never much liked it. *"Get!"* She grabbed a pebble and lobbed it over the shed's roof. It clattered harmlessly. The cat blinked.

She turned back to the grimy little ecosystem at her feet. She plucked up three beetles and two worms. A fat black spider hung off the bottom lip of the path stone, but she couldn't quite bring herself to touch that one.

Once she was back in the shed, she tweezed the beetles' legs away so they couldn't flee—trying not to consider what they thought about that—and then flicked them toward the bat. She skewered the worms on a long splinter and held them out. They wriggled painfully at the end.

The bat examined the beetles, then the worms, then her.

"Come on," she said, waggling the skewer. "I can't sit here all day. Best get a wiggle on and eat."

The bat squeaked. This time she thought she heard anger, or at least exasperation.

"Well," she huffed. "Excuse *me* for livin'. What, you too hoity-toity for a couple worms?"

Squeak.

"Fine," she said, and heaved the splinter at the bat. It landed six inches in front of its nose. "Daddy's waiting on that saw. I suppose you'll eat when you get hungry enough."

The bat squealed.

Dottie Mae dusted herself off and stood.

Daddy was in a brown study over dinner, having not made it as far on the railing as he wanted. And, like always when his mood turned stormy, he complained. Mama ladled out a bowlful of stew and made sympathetic noises while Daddy went on and on about Merle Hackman and how his fence was about to topple over.

"You ask me," he said, mopping up stew with a chunk of hard bread and shoving it into his mouth, "it's 'cause of them two big dogs a-his that the thing's falling down. I call them a menace. If'n one finds its way up here, I'm liable to just bed that sumbitch down—"

"Language," Mama said. Daddy grunted and kept going.

Dottie Mae hardly listened. She thought about the bat. Thought about the silky sheen of its fur, and the matte leather of its wing. She thought about the way its fleshy nose looked like someone had cut it with a knife and pinned the skin flaps back to its snout. She thought about its black eyes like polished stones. They seemed empty, except she knew they weren't.

She'd never seen a bat like that before. It seemed as alien to this place as a giraffe or a kangaroo or any number of odd creatures she'd only encountered in books. She knew she ought to tell Daddy, ask him if he had a notion where the blasted thing came from, but she didn't dare. He'd just go out there with a shovel and smash it to pudding.

"Dottie Mae, you're hardly even picking at your stew," Mama said eventually.

"Sorry, Mama," Dottie Mae muttered. "I guess I just ain't hungry—"

"'I'm *not* hungry,'" Mama corrected. "And we don't do away with good food around here. What, are we just to toss it to the buzzards?"

"Sorry, Mama," Dottie Mae repeated, and forced a spoonful into her mouth.

Dottie Mae snapped awake, her head filled with whispers. Whatever the dream was, it tried to cling to her but its hands were slippery. All she remembered was a grinning mouth with lush, wet lips and a split-open, bloody nose.

It's still hungry, she thought, and—maybe it was still just part of the dream—she thought she knew what it wanted. In the morning she would ask herself if it really happened. But right then, in the cabin's plutonian dark with Daddy's dry snores the only sound, it made perfect sense.

She threw her blanket back.

The moon was full and the sky was clear. It was cold, but Dottie Mae hardly felt the frosty pinch as she drifted up the path. The tom crept ahead of her, a woodrat's body clutched in its mouth. He heard her coming and shot off into the brush.

The shed door hung ajar. Dottie Mae must have forgot the latch after she put the saw back. Except, she was sure she didn't. Whatever lay beyond that black sliver exerted a quiet but steady force, reeling her implacably forward.

The bat had pushed itself deep into the corner. She could hardly see it in the dark, but she could feel its feverish animal heat. She imagined it lying prone against the boards, one wing extended and the other bunched at its side. Its little chest heaved in and out as its agonized body gulped at the fetid air.

Poor thing, Dottie Mae thought. "Shhhh," she said, even though the bat hadn't made a sound. She sat, cross legged, at the ragged edge of shadow.

At first there was nothing. Then little claws scrabbled toward her...*click click click*. She couldn't quite see it, but she felt it wriggle into her lap. It was heavier than she expected, and its fur was just as soft as Mom's old foxtail shawl she kept buried at the bottom of her wardrobe.

It burned like a furnace. She rolled up the sleeve of her nightdress, and that strange nose nuzzled against the crook of her elbow. It was dry. *So* dry.

And then.

Teeth.

Dottie Mae woke up listless and cranky, with a needle of a headache between her eyes. When Mama went to get her out of bed, Dottie simply buried herself in the covers with a mutter.

The blanket whipped back, and Dottie Mae felt Mama's cool palm press against her forehead. Moments later, Dottie heard her whispering to Daddy from the other room: "You best go fetch the doctor from town. It's like she's afire beneath her skin."

Daddy grumbled. Dottie Mae couldn't hear the words, but she imagined the gist. He wanted to keep working on the railing.

"And what'll you tell the Lord on your Judgment Day when He asks why you let your daughter die of the dysentery?" Mama hissed.

"Quiet now," Daddy growled. "You'll scare the girl."

Dottie Mae drifted off again. Sometime later she felt Sparky press his cold, wet nose to her cheek. He snuffled into her ear until she pushed him away, then lay down at the foot of her bed with a thump. Some time later, another palm—this one as hard dry as a scarab—pressed against her forehead. She smelled tobacco and whiskey and something fouler beneath that reminded her vaguely of the shed. It was old Doc McCarty. He always stunk like booze and that other thing, that death thing. Dottie Mae hated when Mama made her go see him.

Doc McCarty poked and prodded, peered deep in her eyes, made her stick out her tongue and say *"ahhhhh."* Dottie Mae obliged, wanting to go back to sleep and escape his stench. The sooner he got on with it, the sooner she'd be shut of him.

"It ain't nothin'," McCarty said to Mama, again in the other room. "Might be a touch of influenza, but she's young and strong and she'll fight it off directly. Just keep her warm and make her drink her broth all the way down, every drop."

Broth, Dottie Mae thought. *Eww.*

With that, she fell asleep.

Wet red lips, an open nose like flayed skin. Black eyes that glistened wetly.

The lips stretched into a crooked, dimpled smile. She was pretty sure these lips belonged to a woman, even though she couldn't rightly make heads nor tails of the face. Every time she tried to focus on the woman's features, they went all fuzzy, like looking through a veil of tears.

But the smile. She saw the smile clearly. And all those white teeth, needling to dagger points. Something in that beautiful, terrible smile stirred something in Dottie Mae. She felt a loose wetness in her down belows, a not unpleasant heat that cooked out of her midsection like she'd swallowed a coal.

She wants, Dottie Mae thought.

She wants...

The bat was gone. In its place was...

...well, she didn't rightly know *what* it was.

It bulged out of the shed's back corner like a wasp's nest. But Dottie Mae didn't hear any buzzing, and anyway it didn't have the papery look she'd come accustomed to. Rather, it looked leathery and smooth, almost like a cow's udder, but marbled black and brown in the lantern light.

A cocoon, she thought. But bats didn't make cocoons. Did they? She realized she didn't actually know much about bats at all. She wanted to ask Daddy, but then Daddy would want to know *why* she was asking, and she'd either have to make something up or tell him, and then it would be the shovel and whatever was left once it was over and done with.

"Are..." She licked her lips. "Are ya in there?"

No answer from the cocoon thing. But something scraped at the back of her mind, itched at it like a probing feather, and she felt all that slushy warmth again and, it seemed to her, she could hear the whispering again.

Her mind went black with it.

It wasn't until she was stood in the bootyard that the night's chill made itself known. It slithered beneath her nightdress and ran frozen fingers along her shivering skin.

The bootyard never much interested her before. It was just a dusty flat spot atop the ridge that rose above the shed, studded with creosote and few sad bunches of prickly pear. A dozen or so forgotten graves for forgotten people.

But here she was, amongst the headstones under a dark, star-crusted dome of night. The moon painted everything in lambent splashes of silver and blue.

She was all sticky for some reason. Most of it was smeared across her arms and hands, but it splattered the front of her nightdress in crimson globules that were almost black in the frosty moonlight. Some of it had got on her face, and she could smell the rich, salty copper of it. She knew the tang of blood.

Sparky was down below, inside the cabin where she couldn't see, barking his foolish head off. But why wasn't Daddy shouting at him to shut his idiot snout?

Why wasn't Mama coming out to look for her?

Dottie Mae looked at her hands. And there it was: the Arkansas Toothpick. She knew it would be there. Its blade dripped with gore.

She had no memory. It was like a void. A big, whistling suck in the center of her skull.

But she knew what happened.

Because of the whispers.

No, she thought. *Oh, no no no—*

The woman's voice answered—low and raspy, like a saw blade against dry wood:

YES.

Please.

No begging, child. It is too late for such. It was too late when you used that thing to take your pater's head from his neck. When you split your mater open from belly to throat. Even as she shrieked for you to stop.

No!

Yes. And now you will wait there in the coemeterium, in the field of the bones. You may put the blade down, if you wish. I will come to you soon.

Dottie Mae felt tears, cold on her cheeks. They cut lines through the paste of viscera. They turned her vision to a prism. Into a veil of tears.

She set the toothpick atop a headstone.

Sparky yelped.

Something scratched through the creosote. Dottie Mae spun. It was only the tom, scampering off into the rocks with something small in its teeth.

Finally, *she* came out of the cabin like smoke. Beautiful and terrible as Dottie Mae knew she would be. Naked and hairless and almost human. But not human at all. Coated head to toe in Daddy's and Mama's blood.

She glided up the path, past the shed and into the boneyard. Her nose, Dottie Mae saw, gaped like a wound.

She knelt before Dottie and smiled through a mouth of dagger teeth. Her cheeks dimpled. Dottie Mae's tears refracted her into a haze, a hundred glittering jewels. Her stink was awful—blood and heat and death—but there was also something low and sweetly carnal that made Dottie want to crawl inside her.

"Am I the most beautiful thing you've ever seen in the world?" The woman-bat-thing asked. Black eyes slicked across Dottie Mae, lit by moonlight.

"Yes," Dottie Mae whispered. She began to tremble as if her entire body wanted to fly apart.

The woman-bat-thing ran a light finger down Dottie Mae's cheek.

"That's strange," she sighed. Her breath was oddly sweet. "Because you're the most beautiful thing *I've* ever seen. You're so beautiful, Dottie Mae, that it hurts my heart to look at you."

"Please don't kill me."

"Oh, I won't," the woman-bat-thing said. "*They* might, when they find you and see. But not I. I will think of you always, though. Thank you for taking care of me."

The woman-bat-thing extended her long, porcelain neck and kissed Dottie Mae on the forehead. The brush of her lips was light, and left a tingling sensation upon Dottie Mae's skin. It was like a tiny fire.

Later, after they led Dottie Mae up the gallows steps and pulled the sack down over her face, Dottie Mae thought back to that tingle, and the luscious hint of sweetness of the woman-bat-thing's breath.

As the trapdoor opened and the rope whipped tight around her neck, she heard those last six words: *Thank you for taking care of me.* And then darkness thundered in forever.

Somewhere along the Animas Forks Road, a porch railing remains unfinished.

STRAW MAN

PATRICIA THORPE

THE WIND HURLED DUST.

Henry Johnson lowered his head against the grit, his hat shielding his face. The sun hung low in the sky, a relentless orb casting its harsh glare over the parched fields of Willow Bluff. Sand swirled in the air, settling onto the cracked earth like a shroud. In the distance, the desperate cries of crows echoed.

Henry stood in what remained of his field, sweat trickling between his shoulder blades. He hoisted the scarecrow onto the cross, its tattered clothes flapping in the dry wind. Fashioned from old clothes and straw, it was a hideous work, its face a ragged burlap bag that once held feed. He'd glued black coal on for eyes, fashioned a nose cut into a hook from a tin can, and stitched on a sneer of black thread.

"Not gonna work," a voice drawled behind him.

Henry froze for a moment, then continued shoving the scarecrow into place.

"Not gonna keep the crows away."

"Well, old man," Henry said, still not turning around. "I figure it's worth a try. What have I got to lose?" He lashed the scarecrow's arms to the cross with rope, looping the rope around its neck to keep the head up. He adjusted the scarecrow's cowboy hat and stood back to survey his work.

"Scary looking thing, I'll give you that," the old man said.

Henry turned to face his neighbor.

Old Man Sawtelle was bent over his cane. He was so stooped now his body was held in a perpetual bow. Pants sagged on his hips and his ripped flannel shirt waved in the hot wind.

"Crows been at what's left," Henry said. "I gotta try to keep 'em away so we have something. Drought took the rest."

Old Man Sawtelle nodded. "Like that all over the county," he replied. "'Tween the drought and the birds, most will be lucky to hold onto their places another quarter, never mind make it to the end of the year."

A wave of despair washed over Henry, smooth and drowning. *We'll make it*, he thought fiercely, *we have to*. An image of Carrie rose in his mind, her pretty face pinched with worry, her eyes anxious and afraid, baby Jack straddled on her hip. He shoved thoughts of his wife and son away and bent to pick up his tools.

"Scarecrows don't help, especially one like that thing. You ought to take it down," Sawtelle said again. "Fact is, they can do more harm than good."

"And how do you figure that? What harm can a thing made out of straw do?"

Sawtelle didn't answer and Henry glanced up at the older man and did a double take. The old man's skin was gray, his face shiny with sweat, his eyes vacant.

"Sam? You okay?"

Sam's eyes snapped back into focus and he rubbed a gnarled hand over his face. "Heat getting to me, I suppose. And seeing that thing." He gestured at the scarecrow.

"What in tarnation is wrong with you?" Henry asked. "Why's a damn scarecrow got you so riled up?"

The old man fished a bandana out of his pocket. "You weren't here when the last drought hit," he said. "Back in '62. As bad as it is now, I reckon. Crops failing, cattle dying. It was a bad, bad time. You ever hear of Lou Lawrence?"

Henry shook his head.

"Owned your place way back then."

Henry shook his head. "Livingston owned my place."

"Before Livingston," Sam said.

Henry waited. Sam blew his nose into the bandana, took a peek at what he'd expelled, and put the bandana back in his pocket. "Lou Lawrence was a good man, but a bad farmer," Sam said. "He planted corn when he should have planted wheat, put plants in the ground too early or too late. He had a dream of being a farmer, but no notion of what the job actually entailed. Then, in '62, like now, there was a drought and what the dry didn't take, the crows did."

Henry felt that swell of hopelessness wash over him again.

"Lawrence had a young wife and a little boy. Can't remember the child's name now, too long ago and my memory ain't what it once was. Lawrence sunk the last of his money into the ground and prayed for a miracle. Least, that's what he told me. He said he prayed and God gave him an answer. Stop the crows. He whispered when he said it, 'Stop the crows.' *He's gone over*, I thought at the time. *Mind snapped like that hot wind over the dead fields.* Few days later, I was passing by and saw what he'd put up. A scarecrow." Sam gestured at the one behind Henry. "Hideous thing. Looked like the one you done just put up. He'd tied a scythe in its gloved hand. That one arm he let hang free; the other he'd tied much like you did, up on a crossbeam out to its side. Christ like, I remember thinking then, and it filled me with a strange unease. I told him I didn't like it and he laughed, but his laughter was a bark of noise, no joy in it. 'It'll do its job,' he said. Just as he said it, the wind blew and the arm with the scythe in its glove swung forward. I know it was just the wind, but for a moment, it was like that arm wasn't made of straw at all. A crow had been just about to land on the fence and when the arm swung, it gave a startled caw and flew away. Lawrence laughed then, a real laugh. 'See Sam,' he said to me, 'it's working all ready.'"

"And did it?"

Sam looked down at the ground, then raised his eyes to Henry. "It did. For a bit," he said slowly. "It started to look like the little Lawrence family would make it through the winter after all."

Henry bit back the annoyance and decided he'd had enough. "Thanks for stopping by Sam, but I got to—"

"And then he killed them."

Henry felt like Sam had punched him. "What did you say?"

"Lawrence killed his wife and son, then took his own life."

"How—"

"With a scythe," Sam said. "Killed them right here in the field, in front of that thing he'd twisted from straw."

Henry stared at the old man then laughed. "Good one, Sam," he said. "You had me going for a minute. I didn't think you were one for ghost stories but—"

"Ain't no ghost story," Sam said. "It's the God's honest truth. You can ask in town, you want. Some folks here still remember. Lawrence went crazy, most people thought, but me? I always thought it was that thing he'd made."

Henry grinned at the old man. "Good job, Sam. But now that story time is over, I got to get back to work. Thanks for the laugh." He turned his back and gathered his tools. As he threw them in the back of his wagon, he realized Sam hadn't moved. The old man was still staring at the scarecrow.

"You should take it down," the old man said.

Henry climbed in his truck and left without another word.

"You going to push that food around your plate all night or are you going to least try a bite?"

Henry's head jerked up and met the eyes of his wife. Carrie was staring at him, concern marring her pretty features. "Sorry, honey," he said. "Got a lot on my mind."

She held his gaze a moment longer, forked a carrot and fed it to Jack, squirming in her lap.. The baby grinned at Henry, slapped the oilcloth-covered table with delight. Henry used a knuckle to wipe his boy's chin.

"I know it's bad," Carrie said softly, "but, we'll be all right. If worse comes to worse, we can always get on the train, go to my family."

Henry heard the wistful note in his wife's voice and the emotion that swelled in him this time wasn't anguish; it was anger. He clenched his jaw. "We ain't leaving," he said, his voice, low and deep, trembling with rage. "This is our home. And we are staying right here. We just got to get through the next few months."

"But, that's the part that frightens me. What if we can't?"

Without a word, Henry got up from the table, grabbed his hat and slammed the door of the little frontier cabin as he left.

A scythe.

That's what the scarecrow needed.

Henry stood in front of the straw man tied to the posts. The moon was a sliver in the sky. In the dark, the scarecrow looked almost human. A brooding beast, larger than life. Moonlight glinted off its hooked nose, made the black thread of its mouth look like an evil grin. As he looked at the scarecrow's black eyes, a shiver ran down his spine and for a fleeting moment, he felt as if it were watching him back. He pushed the unease away. He thrust his hands into his pants pocket, fingered the tin box of matches that had once been his dad's —the one with the faded Union Pacific logo his father swore brought him luck.

A scythe, like the one that fellow Sam told him about used, that would be just the thing. If he tied it to the hand, and let the arm hang free, the wind could move it. That movement could be enough to save what was left of the crop.

Henry went back to his wagon, got a scythe and walked through the swaying stalks to the edge of his field, his shadow leaching into pools of darkness.

He untied the scarecrow's hand (the left one, because the thought came to him '*He's left handed,*') and he tied the scythe securely in the straw man's gloved hand. When he was done, he stepped back to survey his work.

The blade caught the moonlight, held it. The wind blew and Henry held his breath. The gloved hand moved forward with the wind, making a sound as the breeze whistled against its steel.

Henry grinned. It was going to work. He offered up a silent thanks to Old Man Sawtelle for the story.

The crow was covered in blood.

It lay at the base of the straw man's post, its mangled body covered in flies. Henry stared at it, saw the hole punctured in the thing's chest, his mind curiously blank. After a moment, he got a shovel and scooped up the battered crow. He buried it quickly and by the time he was done he could see Carrie coming across the field, his lunch pail in her hands, baby Jack straddling her hip. He could see her frown as she approached, taking in the apparition that wore his old clothes a little too well.

"I don't like it," she said finally. "That thing looks more like a monster than a protector."

Henry leaned against the shovel, wiped sweat from his brow with the back of his hand and said, "It's just a scarecrow. And it's working. The crows are keeping their distance." And they were.

Over the next few weeks, the crows continued to keep their

distance. Those that ventured too close were bloodied and buried in the back field. With no birds to peck at the corn, the crop thrived. His closest neighbor even called Henry's expected yield "bountiful," envy pricked in every syllable. When he made the trip into town, other farmers asked him what he was doing different, his fields being so fertile. Henry would answer them all the same way: "Hard work and sweat." He didn't miss the looks they threw his way.

Each morning, he found himself standing in front of the straw man, studying the thing he'd made. Had it moved? Was the head lower than it had been?

"Have you heard?"

Henry jumped at the voice and whirled around. "For Pete's sake, Sam! You can't sneak up on a person like that!"

Old Man Sawtelle just stared at him.

"Did you hear?" he asked again.

"Hear what?"

"Billy McCain is missing."

Henry's stomach went cold and hard. "What are you talking about, missing? I just saw Billy day 'fore yesterday."

Old Man Sawtelle was watching him closely. "He ain't come home in two days. Wife is a mess, sheriff got a group looking, but there's no sign of him."

"Maybe he went to Springdale."

"On foot? Thirty-six mile walk?"

"Course not, he'd take—"

"—his horse," Old Man Sawtelle said, "but he didn't take Moonstruck. Told his wife he was going to check his east field and he never come back."

Henry's head automatically turned toward Billy McCain's east field, which bordered Henry's land. The scarecrow stood at the juncture. He looked up at the straw man, and for a second, could have sworn the thing was grinning at him.

Henry swallowed. "I'll come help look for him. Maybe he fell."

Old man Sawtelle nodded. "Could be," he said slowly. "Or could be something else."

"You're getting senile, old man," Henry said, with more bitterness than he'd intended.

He got his horse, started across his land and onto Billy's. The wind shrilled through the stalks of corn. He tied Ghost Rider to a post and decided to walk the rest of the field. From a distance, he could hear men calling to each other. The search party, he figured. For a fleeting moment, he thought about joining them, but something inside Henry said he should search on his own.

Henry pushed aside a row of stalks and looked solemnly at the grain harvester, known as a reaper, in the interrow. The horse-drawn reaper was on its own, no horse to pull it. He looked at the reciprocating sickle bar with its sharp, curved teeth that moved back and forth. He stared at the drawbar and harness that should have been attached to a horse. He studied the reel behind, stared at its horizontal prongs.

And everywhere he looked, he saw blood, pieces of flesh and, at the wagon base, a man's hand. His eyes traveled to the ground and what was left of Billy McCain.

He stared.

And finally went to tell the others there was no need to continue the search.

They called it an accident. A misstep with the reaper. But Henry couldn't unsee that clean slice, or the thing that grinned from his field.

"But what was he doing with the reaper?" some folks asked. The crop wasn't ready for harvest. There was speculation and more speculation but no answer could be found. Billy was buried in his side yard, while his wife wailed and his children sobbed as their man was buried in the dirt he'd worked so hard.

Henry went to the services with the rest, but he didn't see the coffin, or the wildflowers that adorned the church. He saw Billy's hand, cut cleanly off at the wrist.

As if by a surgeon's blade.

Or a scythe.

The scarecrow had moved.

Henry was sure of it. It was more forward, leaning out instead of in. Its head was at a different angle, its free arm dangled, the scythe brushing the ground.

Don't be ridiculous, he told himself, *it's just a thing made of straw and string.*

"Take it down," a voice said behind him.

Henry didn't bother to turn. He voiced the words he'd just thought to himself. "Don't be ridiculous, Sam."

Sam didn't answer but Henry heard him walk closer.

"It's gonna get worse," the old man muttered. "Think about your wife and baby, Henry."

Henry barked a laugh.

"That thing...it's demanding something from you. It's feeding off your land. And now it's hungry. What are you willing to sacrifice for a good crop?"

"Nothing," Henry said harshly. "Nothing but my own hard work and sweat."

Old Man Sawtelle was right next to him now, his arm brushed Henry's elbow. "It's time to burn it, son."

Henry walked away.

The baby was crying.

Carrie mumbled something in her sleep and Henry touched her shoulder. He thought about shaking her awake, but even in the scant moonlight, Henry could see the exhaustion lining his young wife's face.

He slipped out of bed, threw on his overalls and made his way as quiet as he could to his son's room.

Jack was standing up in the crib. When he saw Henry in the doorway, he stopped crying and grinned. Something in Henry's heart shifted and he lifted the child into his arms, cooing "Shhh now, shhh…" He changed Jack's diaper and then carried him downstairs to the living room.

The house looked different in the dark. Familiar shapes turned sharp, hard edges that banged his shins and made him swear. When he walked into the door, he cursed louder and Jack began to cry.

"Now," he said, "don't wake your mama." But Jack cried harder and Henry decided to walk the boy outside. The child loved being outdoors. A walk never failed to settle him.

It was a clear night, the wind a rustle in the fields. Henry intended to walk around the front yard, but instead his feet headed east, toward the once-dying crop that had turned bumper.

He was barely aware of the grass under his bare feet, or the cold chill that seeped through his clothes. In his arms, the baby whimpered, then snuggled deeper into his chest.

It'll be fine, Henry thought. *Everything will be fine.*

A cloud drifted over the moon, turning the night darker still. But Henry didn't need light to move by; his feet knew the path. And only when he was in front of it, did he realize he'd been planning to come here all along.

The straw man stared down at him and now there was no illusion. He grinned at Henry and when the wind blew, its free hand gestured toward the child in Henry's arms.

I'm dreaming, Henry thought and that held comfort. Surely he'd wake up soon. But for now, he was stuck in an uneasy slumber while the straw man pointed a blade at his child. Its black eyes held Henry's, and Henry could read the intelligence in them. Malice emanated from the burlap and flannel, and something else, something like...

"Kindred," it said. Its voice was thick, like pebbles grating against larger stones. "We are kindred."

The wind gusted, and the corn stalks crackled and the straw man pointed again.

Henry bent, put the baby at the thing's feet.

"Henry! NO!" Carrie screamed. Henry barely registered his wife in her dressing gown, clutching at his arm. She lurched around him, bent low to snatch baby Jack from the ground. An unnatural wind blew and the straw man's arm lashed out, the blade glinting in the scant moonlight. It caught Carrie's dressing gown, Henry could hear the fabric tear, but the sound came from far away, like they were all underwater.

It's a dream, he thought again. "Give me the baby, Caroline," he said, and his own voice was distorted and thick.

Carrie clutched the baby to her chest and turned to run but Henry grabbed her arm, whirled her back to face him. "Give him to me."

Carrie was screaming, her mouth was open, he could read the terror in her eyes, knew she was pleading, but those sounds didn't reach him. He barely registered his crying wife. He pulled baby Jack from her arms, she clawed at him like a savage, but the years of farm life had hardened him and Carrie was no match. He pushed her to the ground and she clutched his ankles, trying desperately to pull him away from the straw man's reach.

"Get out the way!" The voice came from a great distance. Henry turned, saw Old Man Sawtell running toward them, a kerosene can banging against his hip.

Baby Jack touched Henry's face with a chubby hand. The softness of his child's fingers woke something in Henry and he shook his head as if to clear it.

Old Man Sawtelle threw the kerosene on the straw man. The thing hissed and twisted, and the old man went to light a match, but his hand trembled. Henry thrust his hand into his pocket and grasped his father's tin of matches. With a flick of his wrist, a tiny flame erupted.

"To the devil," he muttered, and flung the lit match into the bundle of straw. Flames licked at the flannel clothing, as if taking a taste, and then burst into a brilliant blaze. As fire engulfed it, the air filled with unholy shrieks. Henry covered baby Jack's ears. Carrie covered her own.

Henry watched grimly as the fire consumed straw. The flames were an awful purple, a color none of them had ever seen. It hurt his eyes to look at it, but more than that, it hurt his *mind*. Finally, the shrieks died down and the purple sparks turned orange. They stood and watched until the thing was reduced to a smoldering pile of ash.

Just as the sun began to lighten the sky, rain fell, soaking the parched earth.

Henry lifted his face into the driving rain and offered a prayer of thanks to Old Man Sawtelle, to Carrie, to Jack, to God. Gratitude flooded his soul and as the rain splashed the ground around them, he felt the land breathe anew.

But just as the last flicker of flame died, Henry heard a gravely whisper, close to his ear, or maybe inside his mind: *"Kindred."*

And then he heard it laugh.

IT GOES ON ALL FOURS

MICHAEL PICCO

I WATCHED as he wandered into The Blind Toad just past dusk.

I could tell that he'd been on the road for a while. The old cowhand looked weathered, beaten down—rawboned and sun-scorched. I met dozens of men like him during my bartending years at The Toad: rangy, hard working, no nonsense men who plied the desert for a living; men who'd been worn down from years enduring the heat, dust, and wind. He wore a pair of battered western ramblers and a long-sleeved shirt that had faded to a sort of colorless gray under the desert sun.

The drover shuffled over to the bar, his weary shadow tangled in his sullen footsteps. He slouched onto a bar stool and uttered a long, exhausted sigh, pinching the bridge of his nose in his calloused hands.

Before he spoke, the Philco went all staticky, interrupting "Please Keep out of my Dreams."

"Whiskey...double. Neat," he croaked, his voice barely above a whisper.

"Sure thing." I set a tumbler before him and gave him a generous pour. "Tough day, huh? It looks like you've been plumb through the wringer and back again."

He merely nodded and downed the tumbler's contents in a single gulp. He emitted a sonorous belch and started to chuckle. "Thanks..." he mumbled. "Yeah, helluva day. One you would *not* believe."

Just the way he said it piqued my curiosity. I turned off the wireless and leaned in, trying to get a better read on the guy. Up close, you could tell it had been a while since he'd slept...or shaved, for that matter. You could see thick, gray bristles speckling the stubble beneath his eyes. Clearly, he wanted to talk, it was just a matter of loosening up his tongue.

"Oh, I dunno...try me," I offered.

He pointed to his empty glass. "Another?" And so, I tipped the bottle again.

He stretched, and I could hear the tendons in his shoulders shift and pop. "Well, I reckon getting it out will help me to forget." He kinda slurred the last word, but his red-rimmed eyes never wavered. "But, I'll tell you something: you ain't gonna believe it."

I set aside the glass I was polishing and asked: "Why do you say that?"

He shrugged and rubbed his eyes. "Because I hardly believe it myself."

I was working on a sheep ranch out near Tuba City when I seen it. I'd been hired as a caretaker by the family lawyer, mostly to tend the livestock there. The rancher who'd lived out there had passed recently, you see, and his kids were living out of state; so, the probate lawyer called me up and asked if I could look after the place for a while. Now, normally, I don't like that sorta work. After all, it doesn't pay very well, but pickings have been mighty slim lately, so it wasn't like I had a bunch of other jobs lined up.

The lawyer described the work at the ranch as "varied." It mostly involved keeping the animals fed, mending fences, and sprucing up the more heel-worn parts of the place. It wasn't nothing too complicated or particularly difficult, but he guaranteed me at least three months' pay while the estate was settled.

The ranch itself was out in the middle of nowhere—just beyond Coal Mine Canyon—about twenty miles or so outside of Tuba City proper. If you aren't familiar with that area, it's all high-desert plateau bordering the Navajo and Hopi Lands. That's some strange damn country back there, lemme tell ya. It just goes to show what the sun can do if left uninterrupted by anything but the night. Yes, sir... time, heat, and wind have carved them hills and canyons like a knife, leaving the landscape twisted and worn. "Eerie," I guess you might call it.

If you spend any time alone out there, it's easy to see why the Navajo avoid the place. It can be pretty easy to get spooked.

I took the wagon into Tuba City the day before to pick up some lumber, so I managed to get an early start to the day. I had hoped to repair some of the hay bunks and replace a few of the rotten fence posts around the corral before the sun got too bad. Temperatures in the afternoon were tipping well into the 90s, you see, and I wanted to avoid as much of the heat as I could.

This morning, I decided to keep the sheep in their folding pen so I could work without them underfoot. They ain't the brightest critters, you know, but I'd taken a shine to the stupid things. During the last few weeks, I'd even gone so far as to name a few of 'em: Lieutenant Cornelius J. Wool, Major Lambchop, Colonel Rotten Cotton, Sargent Mittens. Out of all of them, though, there's one that was my favorite. He's a real troublemaker: an old wether I call Wild Bill Mutton Chops. Or *Mister* Mutton Chops when he's being ornery! He has a habit of head-butting you whenever you turn your back on him. Every time he knocks you over, he does this little prancing jig like it's the highlight of his day. Seeing that, you can't get mad at the stupid thing.

Yeah...without ol' Mutton Chops, I reckon I wouldn't be talking to you right now.

So, there I am, working away, digging out this stubborn rotten post on the east side of the corral, when I hear this ruckus coming from the sheepfold. Now, if you've ever worked around sheep, you know what they sound like when they get all worked up over something. They don't always bleat and "baa"...no, sir! Sometimes, if a situation gets bad enough for them, they will actually *scream*. It's a strange and bone-chilling sound, those screams. There's an almost human quality to them, you know?

So, I'm out there, listening to the sheep wail and bellow, thinking that maybe a coyote or rattlesnake got into the folding pen. I grab my rifle and beat feet over to the pen, hoping I can get there before one of 'em gets injured or killed. But, as I get closer, I hear this strange laughter mixed in with the sheep's cries. The laughter has this looney quality—screechy and crazed—so, I figure it must be one of the local kids out making mischief.

I round the corner to the barn and catch sight of the herd cowering into the far corner of the fold. They're all huddled together, shivering despite the heat, trying to get away from whatever's harassing them—and rightfully so, too. There, in the center of their pen, stands an enormous black goat. At least, at first I *thought* it was a goat. It was standing up on its hind legs, cackling and thrusting its filthy haunches at the terrified flock. The thing had the sort of hard-on you might see on a Shire or Clydesdale, except that it was blue-black and crusted, head-to-balls, with these scaly gray warts.

The thing's laughter was so strange that for a minute, I wondered if this was some sort of pervert all dressed up in a makeshift goat suit. But, you see, its limbs were all wrong for that. They were long... "spindly," I'd guess you'd say—all fouled with shit and canted backward like you'd see on a deer or an antelope.

I think the beast was so caught up in its bedeviling that it didn't notice me right away. But then, I was so stunned by the sight of it that I was struck speechless. The whole encounter just seemed, *unreal*, you know? It wasn't until I mustered enough spit to curse at the thing that it took any notice of me. I probably should've held my tongue because no sooner did the words leave my lips than that thing spun around on them rangy black hooves of his—faster than a coachwhip on a hot rock!

"Who dares disturb my morning rut?" the thing hissed.

And, I'll tell somethin': whatever that thing was, it wasn't no goat...and it weren't no man neither. Just like its legs, its face was... *wrong*. As I got a closer look at it, it looked like someone's...well, someone's *interpretation* of a goat. Like a man pretending to be a goat, pretending to be a man. It had a half-dozen eyes for one thing, every one as black as pitch; and a muzzle that would've been more at home on a coyote than on a goat. Well, that is, if a coyote had itself a long split tongue. It bared its sharp, yellow teeth at me, and I could feel the sweat on the back of my neck turn ice cold.

"You do not belong here, bilagaana," it growled, locking eyes with me. There was something behind them eyes too...something hateful and unnatural. As I stared into them, they began to radiate a hellish glow, like the fires of hell itself were blazin' behind them! Weirder still: the thing's pupils weren't slit, you see—you know, *rectangular* like a goat's are. No, sir...but, lemme tell ya: they weren't quite human neither.

It was like I was looking into the eyes of the Devil himself!

Every fiber in my being told me to get the hell outta there, but I was finding it harder and harder to get my feet movin'. It was like I could feel something—like a giant hand—take hold of me, lockin' me in place. My legs felt like they was sunk into three feet of wet mud —that's no lie!

As I struggled to get away, I watched the thing's front hooves open...unclenching into black and mangy talons. Even its dewclaws seemed to grow longer, twitchin' and flexin' like a scorpion's tail. It stepped closer to me—crouching down and circling me slow— huffing and snarling at me. I guess the terror took over then, and somehow, I managed to raise my shotgun. As I did, the goat man hissed something vile and unnatural. Somethin' strange, like it was talkin' backwards. Well, something I couldn't quite understand, anyway.

The air around me started buzzing...like it was vibrating, you know? At first, I thought I was hearing cicadas, *thousands* of cicadas just 'buzzin'...buzzin'. The noise kept building to the point where it became downright deafening. I wanted to cover my ears, but my arms wouldn't move! I could feel the base of my skull start to itch and then begin to burn. I know that sounds crazy, but it felt like something was trying to bore its way inside my skull, just *scratch, scratch, scratchin'*, lookin' to find its way in.

And there wasn't nothin' I could do or say to stop it!

Thinking back on it now, it was like I was watching this all play out secondhand. At the time, though, I was finding it harder and harder to think straight—that terrible drone in my head swelling, drowning out all my other thoughts. I fought it—you bet I did, too —with every ounce of strength I had, I fought it! But it weren't no use! I could feel that goat thing gettin' *inside my head*, rifling through my thoughts, taking control of me: body and mind.

The beast tromped closer to me then, watching me as newly sprouted horns curled over its raggedy-ass scalp. It leaned in close and snuffled at me, and I could feel its black tongue flick over my cheek— lapping up the sweat beading there. The thing's dick slowly scraped over my pant leg, bobbing and twitchin' as it did so. The stench rolled off it in waves, like rancid meat doused in horse piss. My stomach lurched and, as God is my witness, I thought I saw that goat man smile. And I knew, *I knew*, it wasn't gonna let me leave that pen alive.

The thing's ragged talons scraped over my shotgun, and it whispered: "You should put that shotgun where it belongs, bilagaana." And you know what? Without making any effort at all and *using just the tip of one claw*, it pushed the stock of my rifle downward until the barrel was done pointed straight up. But it didn't stop rotating until it came to rest right under my chin. No matter how I struggled, I just couldn't stop myself. My own body was betraying me! I couldn't resist. I tried—oh, how I tried! I strained until my arms quivered and my muscles cramped, but it wasn't no use.

Somehow, I glanced down, watching my hand fumble toward the trigger.

"Now...open your mouth!" The goat thing barked. And even though I clenched my jaws tighter than a tree knot, it wasn't a minute before I found the barrel tip sliding over my tongue. The bead done sliced up my kisser something awful. Goddamn, even now, I can't get the taste of gun oil outta my mouth!

I ain't ashamed to tell you that all I could do was weep by then. I ain't never felt so hopeless in all my days.

And as if all that wasn't hard enough to believe...

You see, that awful goat thing had positioned himself between me and the sheep in the pen. It had its back to the herd, you see? That was the only excuse Mister Mutton Chops needed to go plowing right into that goat man's scrawny legs! Squealin' and cursin', the thing toppled, and, just like that its spell on me was broken! I yanked the shotgun outta my mouth, righted it as best I could, and fired point blank right into the goat man's belly!

And I'll tell you something: the best thing about buckshot at that range is that you don't gotta aim it all that well for it to be effective.

The blast hurled the goat man a yard across the hard pack. How it shrieked then—howling and thrashing as it pawed at the wound. I think it was trying to gather its ruptured guts back into its body, but it wasn't no use. Nothing, and I mean *nothing*, could've survived a gut full of buckshot at that range. I ratcheted another round, shuffling around it as it flailed and twisted there in the dust.

"Curse you, bilagaana! Curse you!" the thing's voice howled and whined. "Curse you and the death your kind brings to this land. The Darkness, it comes to reclaim me, but know this: the Shadows that dance within me, they will *endure!*"

A crack appeared behind the creature then—like the air around it had been *broken* somehow. A fracture that was just *suspended* there, like something you'd see looking through a shattered lens. All at once, I hear this low, thundering rumble like lightning striking the mesas. The sound rolls over me, scattering the sheep, but that hateful thing, it don't even flinch. No, sir. Something black and formless reaches out of that rift, peeling back the air like it was the skin of an overripe peach. You know—opening it up nice and wide. The shadow grabs the goat man and drags him into the rift.

Inside that fissure, a hellish fire burned. It felt like I was standing in the heart of the sun. I swear I saw pieces of that awful thing twistin' and meltin', boiling away and dropping off it like fatback. I don't reckon the smell is ever gonna leave me. Gawd A'mighty, that awful stench is seared into my sinuses! That goat thing grimaced at me and collapsed backward onto all fours. Its body ran like spent tallow, and its face buckled and fell away. It scuttled away then, cackling and howling into the flames. I heard its howls even as I watched the last vestiges of its body dissolve away into an oily black smoke.

The rift closed then, echoing through the canyons like a thunderclap. All that was left of the creature itself was a greasy stain on the ground.

The ranch hand paused here. His hand trembled as he reached for his whiskey. He drew a shuddering breath before downing the shot in a single gulp.

"So...what the hell was it that you encountered out there?" I asked quietly.

He shook his head, grimacing as he slammed the tumbler onto the bar. "The Navajo call it a yee naaldlooshii." He paused and tried to force a smile. "That's a mouthful, ain't it?" He shrugged, and I heard tendons snapping in his shoulders. "It's some kind of Navajo boogeyman—*very* bad medicine. Roughly translated, it means 'It goes on all fours.' But, when I told the lawyer what I'd seen out there, he called it something else."

I leaned in closer. "What's that?"

Maybe it was a trick of the light, but I could swear that I saw something squirm beneath his hat, something that seemed to be knitting itself into a clutch of knotted and curled horns. The old cowboy grinned then, his smile growing broader until it nearly swallowed up his face. He leaned backward, his spine snapping and contorting. A long, spindly tongue flicked over his chapped lips as its jaw snapped and reconfigured into a vulpine muzzle.

The thing smiled wickedly and said: "He called it a *skinwalker*."

MOONLIT RECKONING

ED DOWNES

THE RIO GRANDE cut through the desert like a raw wound. Thorny mesquite and sharp rocks threw long shadows across the dirt trail, where a supply wagon rattled under guard.

Bandits struck from the ridges, rifles barking in the dim light.

Bullets punched through wood and flesh; screams mixed with the thud of bodies hitting sand.

From the chaos rose a figure on horseback, coat flapping like crow wings. Elias Blackwood spurred his mount forward, revolver steady in his grip. He dropped two outlaws with shots to the chest, their forms crumpling amid dust clouds. The survivors scattered, but one lagged, horse lame from a stray round.

Blackwood closed in, dismounting with predatory grace. He grabbed the man by the collar, slamming him against a barrel cactus.

"Please, mister," the bandit gasped, eyes wide. "I got kin."

Blackwood's lip curled. His eyes shifted, catching the fading sun in a red gleam. Fangs slid out, bone-white and curved. They drove into the man's throat, tearing through skin and muscle. Blood jetted in pulses, hot and coppery, drenching Blackwood's face and the dry ground below. The victim bucked, hands clawing air as life drained away in wet gulps.

Blackwood pulled back, wiping his mouth with a sleeve. The body slumped, a husk with a ragged neck wound leaking into the earth. He mounted up, vanishing into the twilight as coyotes began their chorus. No witnesses marked his path; the night swallowed him whole, leaving only the echo of that final, ragged breath.

Harlan Wade leaned against a post on the boardwalk, wiping sweat from his brow as the sun set on Rio Perdido's main drag. Dust kicked up everywhere, sticking to his boots and making the air thick. The street looked beat up, with faded storefronts and signs that swung lazily in the breeze. A couple horses stood tied up, tails swatting at flies, while miners dragged by, dirt caked on from the depths of the mines.

Talk was buzzing about the new marshal coming in. Harlan fiddled with his deputy badge, still new enough that it felt heavy on his chest. He'd taken the job after the old marshal up and disappeared out in the scrub. No sign of him, just stories about raiders or maybe something meaner. Harlan aimed to step up, especially because that's what his sister Lily would have wanted. He needed to be solid, what with Pa lost to drink and Mom long buried.

Then came the sound of hooves pounding dirt. A man rode up from the outskirts, sitting high on a dark horse, moving steady over the rough ground. His coat draped down, covering his guns, hat pulled low so nobody but Harlan could catch his eyes—they swept the place like he was sizing up trouble. People started clustering, voices low. "Heard he's from the war," one guy muttered. "Made it through Vicksburg."

The man pulled up right at the jail, swung down easy. He looped the reins and turned to the group. "Elias Blackwood. I'll handle the law here."

Harlan moved up. "I'm Deputy Wade. Good to have you. Things have been dicey lately."

Blackwood fixed him with a look that went right through. "Dicey times sort out who's who, deputy. Build some, crush others." His mouth twitched up, but it didn't reach anywhere friendly.

Harlan gave a nod, brushing off that weird coolness in the evening heat. Blackwood walked by a mirror leaning outside the barber shop—the thing just cracked sharp, though nobody but Harlan paid it mind. Harlan showed him into the jail, mind turning over stones.

What was the deal with this guy?

Harlan shouldered through the knot of onlookers squeezing into the alley behind the assay office, dawn light just starting to cut the shadows. Those flies, man, they were everywhere, diving and humming like a bad dream, and the reek slammed into him raw, like meat gone bad under the sun, mingled with that earthy dampness from the sprinkle they'd had overnight. The miner lay slumped against the bricks, shirt ripped to hell, his skin dull gray, slack as if the fight had left him hours ago.

The deputy dropped to one knee, fanning the bugs off the body with his hat. A big blot of blood had seeped out, turning the ground sticky, with scraps of paper and bottle shards caught in the mess like they belonged. There on the neck, two ugly holes stared back, edges frayed and meaty, plunged in far too neat for a wild animal, but not the slash of a fight knife either. Reminded him of those old stories Pa used to spin about critters in the hills, Harlan thought, his fingers prodding the wounds.

No drag marks. No blood trail from anywhere else. Or he picked the wrong bar brawl. Harlan eyed him and rose, scraping his boot on a rock to clean it. Frontier's no picnic: raiders sneaking over the line, some fever making rounds, or plain old stupidity. His gaze flicked to the street end, where talk of Blackwood hung in the air like smoke. This made three bodies like this in under a month.

Doc Emmett stood, dusting his knees. Blackwood's face flashed in Harlan's mind, that crooked grin, and it twisted something inside, made him vow not to let this drop easy. Blackwood had been out roaming after sunset, calling it rounds. It hit Harlan then, thinking of Lily, how she'd slipped away that one night a few weeks earlier, no note, no nothing, just her shawl left on the porch.

He spotted a boot mark pressed clear in the congealed spot, toe aimed right toward the jailhouse side. He followed a step or two; it blurred in the grit, but looked like it was heading toward the marshal's office. Luck, or something else? But it stuck with him, nagging. Folks were spooked plenty.

"Keep a lid on it," Emmett said low. Harlan muttered agreement, but his head was already turning it over. What marshal worth his salt left prints in a dead man's spill? Yet that doubt sat there, stubborn and cold in the rising day. Harlan stepped out to the road, sun warming his back, chasing off the cool.

Harlan crouched behind a stack of barrels in the moonlit alley, windmills groaning overhead like old men complaining to the stars. The moon hung fat, spilling silver light over the twisted path, where shadows stretched from fences and carts left to rot. Air tasted of dust and iron, that sharp bite from the mill's rust, and every creak made him freeze, thinking Blackwood might turn.

He'd followed the marshal from the jail after spotting him slip out, coat collar up, no lantern. Harlan's hand rested on his revolver, thumb brushing the grip. Something about the way Blackwood moved bugged him, too quiet for a big man, feet barely stirring the gravel. Lily's disappearance kept replaying in his head, that empty bed, her quilt still warm.

Now these other bodies.

If Blackwood had answers, Harlan meant to drag them out.

Up ahead, some drifter stumbled from the saloon, pockets bulging. Another man followed him out, and Harlan caught the flash of a knife in his hand. But before he could act, Blackwood moved forward and grabbed the man's shoulder.

"Thieving's a bad habit," Blackwood said, voice low and even.

Claws—actual claws—shot from Blackwood's fingers, raking across the man's chest, shredding shirt and skin in red lines. Then it happened fast.

Blackwood grabbed his wrist, twisting until the blade dropped. The thief screamed, but Blackwood yanked him close, fangs dropping like switchblades, sinking into the neck with a wet tear. Blood spurted, dark and thick, splashing the wall as the body jerked, legs kicking useless.

Harlan's gut twisted; he bit his tongue to stay quiet. Blackwood drank deep, slurps mixing with the thief's gurgles, until the form went limp, a ragged hole leaking down his front.

Blackwood straightened, sniffing the air. "Who's there, little mouse?" A chuckle rolled out, cold as river stones.

What the hell was that thing doing wearing a badge?

Harlan bolted, boots pounding, mind reeling.

Harlan jerked awake in his cramped room, sheets tangled around his legs like they'd tried to hold him down. Dawn light snuck through the curtains, thin and gray, hitting the dresser where his badge lay dull. The air felt stuffy, smelling of sweat and gun oil from the night before.

Had to be a nightmare, maybe.

He rubbed his eyes, that alley scene replaying in his mind. The fangs, blood, Blackwood's laugh chasing him home. But something was off.

On his pillow, right by his head, sat a finger. Severed at the knuckle, skin wrinkled and pale, nail chipped like it'd scratched at dirt. Bone stuck out jagged from one end, splintered white against the dried blood caked in flakes.

Harlan's throat went dry. And there on the finger, squeezed on tight, Lily's ring. The silver band with the tiny turquoise stone Ma had given Lily years before the fever took her.

He picked it up careful, the thing cold and stiff in his palm, blood crust flaking onto the bed.

The finger, a man's? Maybe. But the ring.

He dressed fast, shoved the finger in his pocket, and headed to the jail. He could picture his sister Lily twisting the ring when nervous, like during Pa's rages. No, the finger was too thick for her slender hands.

"What the hell is this?" Harlan slapped the finger down, ring glinting.

Blackwood sat at the desk, boots up, cleaning his revolver with a rag. The ring was hers, no doubt.

"Looks like trouble, deputy." Blackwood glanced at it, face blank. The room smelled of coffee and leather, morning sun slanting in through bars on the window. "Where'd you find that?"

"On my damn pillow," said Harlan.

Blackwood set the gun aside. "Interesting."

"That's my sister's ring." Harlan leaned in. "I saw you last night."

"Careful, dreams bite back," Blackwood said, his voice dropped low, and for a second, Harlan saw fangs again in his mind's eye, snapping shut.

Heat flushed his face; was he cracking up? Blackwood chuckled.

He needed Maria; her saloon stories about border curses might make sense of this mess. *Hallucinations?*

Harlan stormed out, doubt crawling. Blackwood's words hung like smoke.

Harlan slipped into Maria's back room, the door clicking shut behind him. Air hung thick with whiskey fumes and that faint spice from her cooking, chili peppers maybe, reminding him of Sundays at home before everything went south.

The space was tight, shelves crammed with bottles catching the lantern's jumpy flame, throwing wild shapes on the walls: long arms reaching, faces twisted in pain. Worse.

He pulled the finger from his pocket, set it down with a thud.

"You look like you've seen a ghost," Maria said. She stood by the table, wiping glasses, her dark hair tied back, eyes sharp as she took in his face. She leaned closer, then crossed herself quick, eye locked on the finger, Lily's ring on it.

"Found this."

"Sangre diablos. Blood devils. My abuela told stories from the border, creatures that drink life, leave bits behind to mock the living."

Harlan sat, chair scraping wood. She poured two shots, slid one over. "They come at night, peel skin back layer by layer, expose the red underneath, lap it up while it's still hot, steaming in the cool air. They turn their victims into thralls, empty shells wandering."

Harlan downed the shot, burn steadying him. "Sounds like Blackwood. I saw him. Fangs, claws, the works."

Maria nodded. Harlan tensed, peeking through the curtain.

"Legends say they started with the war, soldiers cursed in the trenches, feeding on comrades. Deserters mostly, damned to roam."

A noise outside, boots on gravel. Gone in a blink.

"We need proof," Harlan said.

With Maria, Harlan crept along the back streets to Doc Emmett's office, midnight pressing in with a desert cool that raised gooseflesh on his arms. The building hunkered low, windows dark except for a faint glow seeping under the door like spilled oil. Harlan knocked light, no answer. He tried the handle; it gave with a click.

The place was a wreck. Papers strewn across the floor, ink bottles smashed, black splatters everywhere. But the real horror sprawled on the desk: Doc Emmett, or what was left. His chest cavity yawned open, ribs pried apart like broken fence slats, guts pulled out in loops that trailed over the edge, slick and steaming in the lantern Maria lit. Blood covered everything, thick puddles reflecting the flame, and the air reeked of copper and bile, so strong Harlan gagged, tasting it on his tongue.

Maria whispered a prayer in Spanish, her hand shaking the light. Harlan stepped closer, boots sticking in the mess. Doc's eyes stared blank at the ceiling, mouth frozen in a scream. The heart was gone, torn out, edges ragged with what looked like teeth marks on the stubs of arteries. A note scrawled in blood on the wall: "Silence is golden; curiosity, crimson."

"Doc knew something," Harlan muttered.

Maria held the lantern as Harlan rifled through drawers. He found a photo in an envelope, faded sepia. Blackwood in uniform, 1863 stamped below. Eyes stared out, like they knew someone watched.

"Same face, same scar on the cheek. Unchanged. And now he's here. Decades later," Harlan muttered. "He's not human."

Maria gripped his arm. Harlan flipped over the envelope, finding a return address of Atlanta, but no letter to explain more. Had there been one? Had Blackwood taken it, or had Doc destroyed it? He pocketed the photo, mind spinning with curses and wars.

Paranoia hit Harlan hard. His alliance was sealed with Maria, but fear gnawed deeper: what if Lily was one of those thralls now?

A shuffle came from the corner, low and dragging. Harlan spun, drawing his revolver. A figure lurched from the shadows—a town drunk named Zeke, who begged coins outside the saloon. But not Zeke anymore. Skin pale as milk, veins standing out black and swollen, mouth foaming red-tinged spit. Eyes empty, hands reaching with nails crusted in gore, save for one finger that was missing.

Maria backed up. "Thrall. Like the stories."

Zeke lunged, faster than a drunk should move, fingers clawing for Harlan's throat. Harlan fired, bullet hitting center mass, Zeke staggering back with a hole oozing dark sludge. But he didn't drop. Kept coming, growling wet and animal.

Harlan shot again, head this time. Zeke's skull jerked, rotting brains splattering the wall, and he crumpled, twitching once before going still. Harlan's hands shook as he reloaded, ears ringing from the blasts. "What the hell? He took two."

Maria knelt by the body. "Partial feed. They rise, serve the master until they're finished off proper." She looked up, face drawn. "Blackwood's toying with us. Knows we're digging. What do we do?"

Harlan holstered the gun, hardening inside. Revenge burned now, for Lily, for Doc, for the town rotting under this curse. But doubt crept too—what if Blackwood turned him next? He grabbed Maria's arm. "We get out. Plan our next move."

They slipped into the night, footsteps echoing faint, but Harlan felt eyes on them, that malevolent presence laughing from afar. The frontier had always been hard, but this? This was something from hell's own playbook.

Twilight clung to the cattle trail like a bad omen, wagons huddled in a rough circle against the whipping winds that howled through the badlands. Dust swirled in eddies, stinging eyes and coating throats, while the lowing of steers mixed with the crackle of campfires sputtering down. Harlan rode point with Blackwood, rifle across his lap, Maria back in town but her warnings ringing in his ears—thralls, curses, a monster in marshal's clothing.

There were bandits in the area, or so the trail boss had heard. Blackwood had been hired as protection, and Harlan tagged along to keep an eye on Blackwood. The herd stretched behind, a dark mass under the fading sky, horizon bleeding red like an open wound.

Shouts erupted from the ridges. Bandits charged down, horses thundering, guns blazing. Bullets whined past, punching into wagon wood with thunks, splintering crates. A driver toppled from his seat, chest blooming red, rolling under hooves. Harlan dismounted fast, using a wagon for cover, firing back. His shot caught one rider in the shoulder, spinning him off his mount.

Blackwood leaped into the fray, coat flapping, revolver barking. He dropped two with headshots, bodies hitting dirt hard. But then he closed on a third, grabbing the bandit's arm, wrenching it back with a snap of bone. The man screamed; Blackwood's hand shot up, fingers curling into claws that hooked under the jaw, yanking down. Flesh tore free with a rip, exposing bone and tendon, blood gushing in sheets that soaked the ground muddy. Fangs plunged into the raw neck, sucking deep as the victim thrashed, screams turning to bubbles through the mangled throat.

Harlan froze mid-reload, bile rising. Blackwood fed openly, glancing momentarily at Harlan, no shame. The body convulsed as he drained the life out of his victim. Around them, the fight raged— bandits circling, drivers returning fire, one wagon catching flame from a stray torch. The bandit leader yelled orders from horseback, mustache wild, scar across his cheek from some old grudge.

A shape shambled from the scrub, not bandit, not human. Lily. Or what passed for her. Face gaunt, eyes hollow black, mouth smeared with dried gore, clothes torn. She moved jerkily, hands outstretched, nails caked in filth. "Har...lan," she rasped, voice like gravel.

No. Harlan's world tilted. He remembered her braiding flowers when they were kids, laughing at Pa's tall tales. Now this abomination. She came closer and lunged; he dodged, grabbing a broken stake from the wagon wreckage—sharp wood from a snapped axle. "I'm sorry," he muttered, driving it into her open mouth with a squelch, black ooze erupting around the wound, spraying his shirt.

She crumpled, gasping once, then lay still. Harlan yanked the stake free, slick with ichor, tears blurring his vision.

Blackwood wiped his mouth, stepping over his victim. "Family reunions. Messy, ain't they?" A grin, fangs retracting with a click. In Harlan's mind, a flash: Blackwood in war fog, kneeling at a ritual fire, shaman's chant turning him, curse sealing in smoke. Gone quick, but it hardened Harlan's hate.

Blackwood walked to his horse and swung into the saddle. "Who's gonna believe what you saw here, deputy? Best to just forget."

Amid the dead, Harlan questioned everything—justice, monsters, his own breaking point. The west had chewed him raw.

The next night, Harlan rode out to the mission ruins as dusk settled, the adobe walls crumbling into the sand like forgotten bones under a sky streaked purple and gold. Cacti dotted the path, spines catching the last light, while tumbleweeds skittered ahead, driven by a wind that moaned through the gaps in the old bell tower. The place felt cursed, Spanish crosses leaning crooked, ground littered with pottery shards that crunched under his horse's hooves. He dismounted, tying the reins to a rusted gate, mind turning over the plan.

He'd forged the letter back in town, ink smudged on cheap paper: "Meet at the mission. Got info on your past. Come alone."

Signed it from Doc, knowing Blackwood would bite. In his pocket, the photo from Emmett's office burned as proof—same man, decades before. Harlan loaded his revolver with silver bullets Maria had melted from church candlesticks, the metal heavy and cold. A wooden stake from a fence post was tucked in his belt, tip sharpened.

For good measure, he tested the holy water vial on Zeke's severed finger, saved from the office mess. A drop hit; flesh hissed, bubbling and melting in pinkish strings, reek of charred meat filling the air. Worked. But doubt nagged— what if this turned him into a monster too? Lily's face flashed, her final rasp echoing.

Wind picked up, carrying a low laugh from the ridges. Shadows grew long, twisting into shapes that murmured doubts: *Join us. Easy power.* Harlan shook it off, steeling for the trap. Blackwood would come; question was, who would walk away?

Harlan waited inside the mission church, moonlight pouring through broken stained glass, turning the flagstones into a patchwork of colors gone wrong, a tapestry of blues bruised and reds like fresh cuts. Altars hunkered in the corners, vines choking the stone, air thick with dust and the faint rot of old incense.

Wind rustled through, carrying a chill that didn't match the desert night.

"A note in Doc's hand?" Blackwood emerged from the archway, coat billowing, steps silent on the cracked floor. "Clever, deputy."

"What are you?"

Blackwood circled slow, scars on his face shifting in the light, almost moving, like worms under his skin from some old hex.

"What am I? A soldier once, bitten in Vicksburg's mud."

"End this." Harlan gripped his revolver, stake heavy at his belt.

"Or maybe I made a deal with border spirits, blood for eternity. Pick your poison."

Harlan raised the gun. Blackwood's laugh cut sharp, eyes reflecting moonlight like coins of a greedy ferryman.

"You killed Lily!"

Blackwood lunged, claws out, slashing Harlan's arm.

The vampire hissed, delight in his grin. Pain flared; Harlan fired, bullet grazing Blackwood's side, black fluid seeping.

"It's starting. Feel that burn?"

Harlan backed up, mind flashing to Pa's war stories, moral lines blurred in battle. Was Blackwood victim or villain? No time; fear fueled him now, raw and personal.

Gunfire cracked the air, echoes bouncing off stone altars as Harlan squeezed the trigger again, bullet slamming into Blackwood's shoulder. Black ichor exploded out, chunks of meat and bone flying, but the wound knit back with wet snaps, flesh reforming in twisted ropes.

Blackwood roared, charging low, claws raking Harlan's thigh, tearing muscle deep, blood pouring hot down Harlan's leg.

Harlan stumbled back, firing wild, one round clipping Blackwood's ear, lobe shredding in a spray. Pain screamed through him, but he circled, using a fallen cross for cover.

Something moved behind Blackwood. He whirled, grabbing her by the throat, lifting her off the ground.

"For...the blood...you've spilled!" Maria choked out as she fought for life.

Maria gasped, eyes wide, fingers scrabbling as crimson bubbled from her mouth. She stabbed a crucifix into his arm; skin sizzled, blisters rising fast, but he snarled and hurled her onto a rusted spike from the ruined railing. It punched through her gut with a meaty thunk, blood sheeting down her dress, organs sliding slick along the metal.

Harlan lunged, stake in his fist, driving it into Blackwood's back mid-turn. Harlan twisted the stake deeper, feeling the wood grind against bone.

"No!"

Blackwood convulsed, spewing more fluid in arcs. His body arched and he howled, hands clawing at the air as he spun, fangs grazing Harlan's neck, sinking just enough to tear skin, venom burning in. Wood crunched through Blackwood's ribs, piercing a lung with a pop, dark gore fountaining from the entry.

Maria wheezed her last breath. Blackwood slumped to his knees, whispering guttural curses. War chants, maybe, from that cursed field. Victory tasted sour. Harlan yanked free, stake dripping, bite mark throbbing fierce.

Harlan staggered from the mission ruins into the pre-dawn desert, legs heavy as lead, the vast sands rolling endless under a graying sky. His boot caught on a rock; he nearly fell, catching himself on a cactus spine that drew fresh blood from his palm. The bite on his neck pulsed hot, veins crawling like roots under his skin, spreading a fire that no water could quench. He touched it, fingers coming away slick, dark lines threading up his arm now, visible in the weak light.

A puddle from some rare rain mirrored his face—distorted, eyes shadowed, but the reflection warped further, fangs peeking from where his gums ached sharp. He blinked; it steadied, then flickered again. Hallucination? Or the curse taking hold?

Shadows shifted behind the crumbling walls, a faint laugh riding the wind—Blackwood's?

The west stretched merciless, promising no end to the hunger building inside, a gnawing that whispered temptations of power, of feeding under stars.

Harlan froze, breath ragged. His fangs itched fuller now, the cycle reborn in him. Dawn edged closer, but the dread swallowed it whole —what monster walked away tonight?

SAGUARO MADNESS

RICHARD LAU

CROSSING a desert with a posse of lawmen and angry townsfolk on your tail ain't a whole lot of fun. The heat, the snakes, and the other varmints don't make things any easier, either. But now in addition to all that, apparently I was out in the company of a madman.

"I tell ya, Petey, it's the same cactus. The same goddamned cactus!"

Keeping my hat brim pulled low, I gave my partner-in-crime a sideways glance, and I'm sure my horse did, too. I noted he still had both hands on his horse's reins, away from the holster on one of his hips and the machete on the other.

That was a good thing...for him. I had long adjusted to riding with my drawing hand resting casually on my upper thigh, so as not to attract any unwanted attention by shifting my position.

The man next to me called himself Jake Corbitt, but who really knew? He admitted he got a kick out of seeing different names above his face on the various wanted posters. He even collected them, which would be to his detriment if he were ever caught. And though he didn't plan to be taken in alive, the thought of making some bounty hunter rich still irked him like a rattler under his boot. Anyway, whoever he was, my brother of stagecoach, bank, and homestead robberies had apparently two-stepped over the edge of a very tall cliff.

Saguaro madness, they called it. Cactus fever. Loco from the poke-ohs. Call it what you will. The ailment probably had more names than Jake himself. Spend too long in the desert, and you start imagining things about them spiky plants, giving them all sorts of human behaviors and characteristics.

I had heard about a man who'd gone crazy thinking that them cactuses had eyes and were staring right back at him. Even at night with his own eyes closed. A wagon train woman went hysterical, swearing she saw them change their shape. The Indians have similar tales, too.

If you're not careful, the desert will sneak up on you like a rattler that refuses to rattle. Once it gets its venom into you, your own poisoned mind becomes your worst enemy.

Jake's particular fixation? He claimed that we'd passed the same cactus five times already.

I knew we weren't riding in circles. While Jake was staring at the multitude of cacti, I was using the one and only sun as our guide. Every daybreak and sunset told me we were going in the right direction, and that was good enough for me. The world would have to go mad for the sun to be wrong.

When I tried to explain this to Jake, he replied, "If we're not going in circles, then it must be following us."

I pointed out that his favorite cactus, if it was indeed the same one, was always appearing in front of us, not sneaking up from behind.

We both had been watching over our shoulders for the telltale dust clouds of the pursuing posse and hadn't seen any cactus following on horseback or otherwise. Furthermore, we had been zigzagging randomly, so how could the cactus know how to get ahead of us?

Jake was still not convinced. "Maybe it just knows where we're headed, where we're going to be heading. Or it could just be guessing and getting really lucky. It's getting ahead of us somehow."

Now I ask you, what fella in their right mind thinks like that and then actually says such a nutty thing aloud? I'll tell you who. Someone who is crazy, or close to getting there.

Of course, how certain was I about myself, my own thoughts and judgments? Why was I even trying to use logic with Jake's crazy proposition?

That's what the desert does to you. It makes you think. Think too much about the wrong thing, and you end up like my partner. Or like me, if I didn't watch out.

Saguaro madness was contagious.

Instead, I thought about our partnership. How long it should go on, if it should go on.

If one was to be cold hearted, I mean, rational about it, Jake still had his uses. If the posse ever caught up to us, we could split up. The posse would end up chasing just one of us, and, if I was lucky, it wouldn't be me. If we made it across the border, sometimes Mexico wasn't the friendliest of places for gringos. Especially for ones in our profession. The citizens don't want any more lawlessness, the Mexican authorities want you for the wrong reasons, and the local bandits just want you dead. In that situation, it's good to have a second gun and second pair of eyes handy.

The ill-gotten gains tucked in our saddlebags wouldn't last forever. If there was another round of robberies, how hard would it be to find and break in a new partner?

Of course, just being around Jake in the best of times was risky. Maybe I had gotten used to it, numb to the danger? But now Jake was looking and sounding more and more dangerous, like a horse had kicked him in the head, and now everyone, including me, including the cactus, were looking like horses.

Jake and I had very different temperaments. I was more of a planner, a thinker, quiet and bookish looking. He was impetuous, given to sudden dives of passion and violence like buzzards spotting a fresh corpse.

But that volatility was why I needed him. If I rode into town with a Gatling gun hitched to the back of a wagon and threatened to kill everyone, the town's kids and womenfolk would laugh me off. All it took from Jake was a squinting glance, a growl from the gut, and an occasional wad of spit for emphasis. There was no doubt any further argument would be punctuated with a bullet.

The only things we had in common were the need for money, a desperation to get it, and the inability to hang on to it for long.

We had been riding full steam for six days from our latest thievery in lower Arizona, trying to cut across Southern California into the relative sanctuary of Mexico. But the border seemed to be riding a horse of its own, constantly galloping away from us.

We had ridden this route before, with slight variations. When you have the Law on your trail, it never pays to be too predictable. I didn't have an explanation for why it was taking longer this time. Were we really lost or was Jake's panicky delusion just playing into that impression?

There was a balance to be found, but like the border, I had no idea where it was.

Jake pulled up suddenly, his tired horse welcoming the rest. I figured mine could use a break, too. But when I saw what he was gawking at, my shooting hand slowly moved toward my gun butt.

Jake was staring down the cactus in front of us.

It was an imposing ten-footer, a solid center torso with two thick arms rising up. It amused my outlaw heart to think it resembled a victim of one of our many hold-ups, giving the universal sign of surrender. I had to admit that this cactus did resemble Jake's nemesis, but many of them grow to that size and shape.

Jake slid out of the saddle, and from my years of working with him under stressful circumstances, I knew something was about to happen. It's the feeling you get when you sense an approaching thunderstorm. It felt like right before he shot the unarmed bank clerk just for the hell of it, or the stagecoach driver who had already thrown down his guns.

If he turned on me, I'd deal with him like a lame horse. But I wasn't about to tip my hand.

I didn't need to worry. Jake's attention and anger were reserved for the cactus. He slipped out his machete and with one swing, sliced off the top fifth of the center column.

I felt a little squeamish watching the violence, even if the victim was just a saguaro. The white man hasn't been around long enough for the cactus to be anything more than a change in scenery or convenient target-practice for pistol or piss. You can't even drink the water out of the damn things without getting sick.

But the Natives, who have lived among these plants for thousands of years, pay them great respect and hold them sacred, viewing them as spiritual ancestors. I nervously glanced around, worried that some Native eyes were witnessing this sacrilegious slaughter. We didn't need any more trouble.

"There!" Jake growled. "Let's see you follow us when ya got no head!"

He gave me a gap-toothed grin of triumph as he hopped back in the saddle. I quickly raised and waved my hat, whooping and hollering in shared triumph, hoping I sounded sincere and supportive.

I also hoped he didn't notice that I had been ready to draw on him.

It looked like my old buddy was back. If this was all it took to improve his mood, the rest of our journey should be a smoother, more enjoyable ride.

We rode until sundown, with no further sign of Jake's tormentor. We made camp with not a single cactus in sight. Just a waterless beach of sand.

I thought the paranoid cactus talk had been dropped, but Jake's final words of the night were, "See? I told you. It can't follow us with no head."

"Whatever you say, Jake," I mumbled grumpily, hunkering down in my bedroll. It was going to be a long night, and I wasn't planning to sleep.

I must have dozed off. Because you don't dream when you're awake, right? You don't have a nightmare about being slowly surrounded, of being the focus of a hatred with the intensity of the midday sun.

I awoke to the feeling of spit hitting my face. But it wasn't spit; it was rain.

Rain!

"Jake!" I yelled. "Get up! It's raining! We can fill the canteens!"

It wasn't raining; it was storming. I rushed to my saddlebags, my mouth opened and upturned to capture the falling drops of sweet moisture. The rain was really coming down, and I turned my hat upside-down to collect more water.

"Damn it, Jake!" I called to his still figure on the quickly dampening ground. "Get up and help me!" I moved between the horses, intending to get Jake's canteen as well to fill it up.

Lightning lit up the night and thunder rolled. I'd been in my share of monsoons, but nothing like this. This run for the border was really cursed and getting worse every second. The horses were whinnying, rearing up on their hind legs, and it was all I could do to hold desperately to the reins.

"Jake! You lazy sonovabitch! Get up! The horses are bolting!" My shouting over the wind probably panicked the horses even more.

My partner remained motionless, hat pulled down over his sleeping face like a passed-out town drunk. My temper got the best of me. Since he wouldn't go to the horses, I dragged the horses over to him. The animals felt better moving, thinking I may be leading them to shelter.

Instead, I hauled back my foot and gave my partner a full kick in his crossed boots.

That's when the rain stopped suddenly, as if it was shut off at the pump. The thundercloud curtain parted, giving way to the light of a full moon. It was as if I had a bright lantern over my shoulder, over the entire desert, in fact. Flash storms were often like that.

But what wasn't common was what I saw when I kicked Jake's boots to wake him up. His hat fell away, off his shoulders, and, with reins still loosely in hand, I kneeled over and retched as if I had swallowed a bellyful of rotgut. Jake's neck ended in a ragged, bloody stump. I couldn't help but be reminded of...

I was being watched.

I rose, turning slowly, reaching for my six-shooter, uncertain that it would do any good. But there was a comfort knowing it was there, like a terrified little boy hugging his teddy bear for what imaginary protection it could provide.

My heart bucked like a bronco. About twelve feet away stood a cactus.

"*The* cactus," I could hear Jake's voice whisper in my head.

But was it the same cactus? This one was different. Its two arms pointed downward, as if in a gunfighter's stance.

But with the full moon overhead, there were no shadows, and I could clearly see that its center column had been recently damaged and split. And wedged snugly between the two divided sides rested Jake's head. I stared into his horrified expression one last time. It was the only time I ever saw regret and sadness in his unblinking eyes.

The cactus slowly raised its left arm, and the moistened glint of the machete's blade glistened in the silvery moonlight. Gone was the hapless hold-up victim. In its place, a furious pig butcher.

I stumbled toward the horses, the world spinning in one direction, me in another.

But my dizzying vision still made sense of one thing: Jake's cactus had brought friends.

I leapt on my startled, neighing horse, dug in my spurs, and rode the hell out of there.

And behind me, I swear I heard the damned saguaros whooping as they chased after me.

THE RATTLER'S BRIDE

J.R. TAYLOR

THE TOWNSFOLK WOULD LATER SAY the snake was an omen. Sent by God as retribution, a punishment for her sins. Others whispered it had to be the Devil, come to fetch his own. Some would scoff at these claims and call it nothing more than bad luck. But Clara Cartwright knew the truth.

The snake didn't just strike. It chose.

It was the sixth day of August when Clara walked out into the desert behind the church, a pistol in one hand, her ma's wedding veil in the other. The veil was an heirloom, meant to be worn twice – but it had only crowned the brow of one bride, long since buried.

Clara never did get her turn to wear it.

As she walked, her boots crunched across the dry landscape, the ground marked with cracks in the hard-packed earth as though something from down below had been pressing up, trying to get out. Her feet struck up clouds of dust, puffs of red curling away into the air. The heat clung to her like a fever—heavy, inescapable, breathless—and the sun reached down from the punishing sky with long, blistering fingers, as if trying to peel the very skin from her bones.

Clara squinted across the shimmering horizon, the view wavering like a mirage in the heat. A lone buzzard circled slow and wide over the craggy spine of the mountains beyond.

Clara licked her dry, chapped lips and turned her face upward. Even the sky seemed brittle, the blue pale and dusty as though it had been faded with bleach. Not one cloud interrupted the vast blue expanse—not even a hint of mercy against the brutal and unforgiving sun.

She'd gone there to die. Not with a note, not with any sort of drama. Just the quiet resolve of someone already buried by shame.

It had been one month since Caleb Dorsey cornered her behind the chapel pews and whispered sinful things in her ear with whiskey on his breath, as she pleaded first for him not to...then for him to stop...then to God for forgiveness.

One month since her father, the preacher, spat the word *whore* through a mouthful of scripture.

One month since the good, god-fearing rancher she was meant to marry had broken his promise—a sneer on his lips as he labelled her spoiled goods.

She looked down at the veil in her hand, her fingers tracing the delicate fabric. The lace, once white as snow, had yellowed with time, but still felt soft as a whisper in her hands.

Out of nowhere—as if on purpose, like a final twist of the knife, a gust of wind rose— dry and spiteful, snatching the piece of cloth from her clutches. With a gasp, she grabbed for it, stumbling forward, but the veil flew farther with every step, swallowed by the yawning expanse of desert before her.

She fell to her knees—not in grief, no. That had long since run dry. Just in simple, aching defeat.

If God wanted to wash me clean, she thought, *wouldn't he have sent rain? Wouldn't he have answered my prayers?*

But whatever power was listening at that moment didn't send rain.

Instead, it sent the snake.

The sound was subtle at first—like a hushed breath, quiet as a soul slipping out of a body.

Then it was there.

A Diamondback, thick as her forearm and long as a rifle. It rose from the dust, its head reared back, regarding her with eyes hot like coal.

Clara didn't scream. She didn't move.

She met its gaze.

They held there for what felt like an eternity, a girl and a serpent, breathing in the same dust. And in that stillness, something old passed between them.

Maybe this was her sign from God. Maybe this was his messenger, sent to take her home.

The snake raised its head, its forked tongue flicking in the air, as though testing her.

She closed her eyes. She folded forward as if in prayer, not cowering in fear, but rather making an offering. And she waited for her fate.

The bite was clean, two needle-like pricks in the center of her wrist.

She did not cry out. She did not feel fear. She welcomed the ending. Slower than a pistol, but cleaner.

The world tilted. The horizon, already shaky with heat, swelled and distorted before her eyes. The buzzard cried out once in the distance, its caw echoing in her ears. Clara collapsed into the dirt, the dust rising in waves around her.

And the desert—like God— said nothing at all.

Her father found her hours later, slumped over beneath the long shadow of the chapel. The sun had dragged itself to a new position in the sky, and now the steeple cast her in shade.

The pistol lay untouched in the dirt beside her, half buried by wind-blown red sand. Her arm stretched out before her, her wrist bloated and bruised, but still pulsing like a second heart—the poison claiming her from the inside, the job not done yet.

He stared down at her with a sigh of inconvenience. Disappointed, maybe, that the scavengers hadn't finished the job.

"Damn foolish girl," he muttered. Still, he bent and hauled her into his arms .

Inside the darkness of the house, he laid her on her narrow bed beneath the window, drawing the moth-eaten curtains closed against the glare of the late afternoon sun. He pulled a blanket over her—maybe for warmth, but more likely as a shroud.

He did not speak her name. He did not pray.

But as he turned to leave, Clara's eyes opened, fluttering like the wings of a moth.

"Please," she whispered, barely more than a breath, her lips hardly moving at all. She fumbled weakly beneath the blanket, her hand finally untangling from the white sheet and reaching for her father like a child.

"I don't want to die alone," she rasped.

He paused for a moment, just long enough to make her hope. And then he walked away, closing the door behind him .

Night fell.

The fever opened in her, heat swallowing her alive, her body burning with the licking tongues of hellfire, her blood boiling. Sweat poured down her brow. She was burning alive—not on the outside— deeper.

In her bones.

In her soul.

Her skin itched with invisible crawling things, but no matter how desperately she clawed at her arms, her legs, her face, it wouldn't stop.

Somewhere deep in the marrow of her bones, the venom

bloomed and spread its roots into her veins, while the fever cracked open her skull and welcomed visions inside like old friends.

She dreamed of sermons swallowed by flame, of her father's mouth screaming psalms, spitting saliva that burned like acid. She saw Caleb, his larger, stronger body crushing her down, sweating on top of her, his face melting into something inhuman, his mouth stretching wide and sharp with glee, growing wider as she screamed and screamed. Her mother's voice called her name from the corners of the dark, but when Clara reached for her, she turned to smoke in her desperate hands.

The air stank of sickness—sweat and blood and piss and something else: something darker and ancient and foul.

Her spine buckled. Her body writhed and twisted, the bed frame groaning in protest. Her muscles screamed. Her bones cracked. Her jaw stretched wider than should have been possible. But she could feel it—her body was not breaking. It was becoming something else.

The fever burned through the night and bled into the next day. Time bent. Shadows lengthened. Light crawled across the floor, dragging itself forward hour by hour as the sun made its journey from the east to the west.

She fell deeper into the dream. A grave. Dirt rising all around her. Her father loomed above her, looking down with disdain, his body blocking out the sun. She yelled for him, screaming that she was still alive as he tossed shovels of dirt over her, her mouth filling with earth, worms wriggling against her teeth.

Hands rose beneath her, long and sharp and hungry. They grabbed at her ankles, her wrists, her hair, dragging her down, down, down.

And then...silence.

Sudden, consuming silence, so deep it felt like drowning in an endless sheet of black velvet.

The hands released her.

From the darkness, a figure emerged, wrapped in shadow. It watched her, a faceless thing, but she felt it watching. And like the snake, something passed between them. An understanding.

A voice of shadow and bone, of fire and ash, whispered from all around her, a quiet, hissing echo that blew across the room. The figure had no face, no mouth to move, but Clara knew the words came from it, reverberating in her mind. Had it been spoken aloud? Or had it simply wormed its way into her head?

Do you wish for rest, girl?

Or do you long for vengeance?

Clara did not hesitate.

Vengeance.

And the deal was done.

A force yanked her backward, and with a start she awoke back in her bed, her body swallowed by agony.

Her skin blistered, split, and peeled away from her body like strips of paper. She opened her mouth to scream, but her tongue split—forking, lengthening, twitching against her teeth like some foreign creature. She gagged on blood.

Her knuckles turned white as she gripped the sheets, her limbs twisting, her ribcage shifting, her body swallowed by the change.

Her spine arched, a sound of cracking splitting the room, lifting her entire body up from the bed, every muscle screaming for relief.

Then, just as suddenly as it came, the fever broke like thunder.

Clara collapsed into the stillness of the night. She lay on the bed, her eyes wide, her chest heaving. The room quieted. The curtains fluttered in the cool night breeze.

And then, from the shadows, it came.

The Diamondback.

It slithered through the open window like a whisper.

Its scales shimmered in the moonlight, glinting like a knife's edge.

It watched her. Its tongue flicked once in the air.

It did not strike. It did not threaten. Now, it knew her.

It slid beneath the bed to wait. To serve.

The next night, her father returned. Outside, the sun had begun its slow descent behind the horizon, painting the sky red as communion wine.

He had come ready to bury her. A shovel in one hand, for the body. A bible in the other, for the soul.

He opened the door with a quiet reverence, like a man entering a tomb.

But Clara was not dead.

She sat upright in the bed, her spine curved and her head bowed low. Her sweat-damp hair hung down in long, tangled strands, veiling her face. The blanket had been discarded on the floor, and at some point during her fevered thrashing, Clara had ripped off her clothes and now was draped in only a thin dressing gown, the fabric sticking to her sweat-slicked body. Her bare arms hung limp at her sides, and in the waning half-light of the early evening her skin shimmered faintly, taught and smooth.

Her father froze in the doorway. The shovel clattered to the ground.

Clara's head tilted to the side—a slow, animalistic movement—turning her ear toward the sound.

Slowly, she lifted her head. From beneath the bed came the whisper of scales. Clara met her father's eyes, and his went wide with shock, his mouth stretching wide, his chest expanding with air, but before he could scream, the Diamondback launched itself forward and struck in a blur of motion, burying its fangs in the soft flesh of the preacher's neck.

He staggered backward, his hands flying to his neck, his eyes bulging wide, rolling in their sockets as if searching for a savior he didn't deserve. The snake released its grip, dropping to the floor. Clara reached down, a tender hand outstretched, and the snake wound itself around her wrist like a bracelet.

As she rose, her father fell to his knees, and finally, his fearful eyes found hers again. Perhaps in those final moments, he saw his daughter. Perhaps in his feverish state, he saw his wife—the one buried so long ago—returned to drag him to his fate.

Clara stepped toward him. He tried to scramble backward, but the wall was already at his back. His breathing was labored. Sweat poured from his brow. It wouldn't be long. His eyes turned toward the heavens.

"God, have mercy," he breathed, the words fighting their way from his fumbling lips.

Clara crouched before him, her movements graceful and serpentine, until she was face to face with her father.

"You ask God for mercy?" she hissed, and the voice that slithered from between her lips was not her own. "God ain't here."

She leaned in, her breath hot on his face.

"But I am."

She smiled, and her teeth were sharp. The preacher's body convulsed, shuddered, and slumped to the floorboards with a hollow thud.

For a long moment, Clara watched him. The snake curled tighter around her wrist, its heart beating in time with her own, the two of them breathing as one.

Eventually, she stood and stepped over the empty shell of her father. There was more to be done.

She shed the spoiled dressing gown, dropping it to the floor. In her father's bedroom, she opened the old chest at the foot of his bed and lifted out a new skin for herself. The silky white fabric of her mother's wedding dress slipped over her body .

She moved through the house like a vengeful phantom, a vision in white, pausing only once to tear down the crucifix that hung over the hearth. It crashed to the stone floor and splintered. She did not look back.

Outside, night had swallowed the desert whole.

She mounted her father's old black mare and rode toward town.

She knew where to find him. That part was easy.

Caleb Dorsey spent every free moment between a woman's thighs or at the bottom of a whiskey bottle: laughing loud, drinking hard, and putting his hands in places they didn't belong. He liked to haunt the brothel at the end of Main Street, where no one had the courage or reason to stop him.

Clara rode the mare through the sleeping town. The bank and general store stood shuttered for the night, the boarding house windows dark. Only the brothel's windows glowed at the end of the street, the lamplight spilling onto the road, the sounds of sin bleeding into the quiet night: the clink of glasses, sloshing over with whiskey, the clatter of coins, and the false laughter of women who were paid to pretend.

The mare's hooves struck the ground with a rhythm like a marching drum, and the snake tightened around her wrist, sensing the coming storm.

She didn't hitch the horse—she wouldn't be there long.

Clara climbed the front steps and pushed open the batwing doors, stepping inside. Cigar smoke and body heat engulfed her, thick with the smell of sweat and perfume.

She sauntered down the center of the room, an omen in white.

The piano slowed, and the laughter thinned as the room took notice of her.

The oil lamps flickered, and her skin shimmered in the dim light. Her eyes burned gold, her pupils slitted and reptilian, scanning the room, seeking their prey.

The crowd parted around her, the men frozen, their faces white with fear. The woman looked on with reverent stares, as though reveling in the presence of a vengeful goddess.

No one moved. No one breathed.

In the back of the brothel, Caleb Dorsey reclined in a chair, facing away from the scene. Shirt unbuttoned, whiskey in one hand and a girl on his knee.

When the piano faltered to a stop with the plink of a wrong key,

Caleb slammed down his glass, still seemingly unaware of the hush that had blanketed the crowd. "Play it again, damn you!" he barked, and turned toward the crowd as if to gain their support. Then, finally, he saw her.

She stood before him, divine and fearsome, with her chin held high. The silky white of her dress shone in the lamplight, and the snake around her wrist rattled its tail. She regarded him like one might regard a tick dug into the skin—with revulsion and resolve.

Caleb paled, the blood draining from his cheeks. He shoved the girl off his knee and stood, too fast, knocking over his chair. His hand flew to the pistol on his belt.

"What are you?" he whispered, backing away, one hand held out in front of him.

Clara tilted her head, studying him. The trembling hands. The sour stink of sweat and liquor. The pathetic quiver in his voice.

This man, she thought, once destroyed her.

But now?

"I am retribution." She grinned, and her forked tongue flashed between her teeth.

She lunged, faster than he could react, her hands slamming into his bare chest. Her long, sharp nails split his skin, and black smoke rose from the wounds as he screamed—or tried to. But her venom was already taking hold. His jaw locked, and his mouth hung open in a rigid, silent howl. His limbs jerked, then stiffened, locking in place like he'd turned to stone. Clara leaned into him slowly, her nails still digging into his chest. He fell back against the wall and slid to the floor, his eyes wild with fear and fixed on Clara as she followed him to the ground.

The Diamondback unwound itself from her wrist and slithered free.

It dropped to Caleb's chest, scaling his ribs, his collarbones, sliding up his chin. Caleb tried to move, to scream, to beg, but he could only watch in horror as the snake raised its head and came eye to eye with the man.

"Ask me not to," Clara said, and smirked at his silence.

The snake swayed, its forked tongue tasting the air. And then, it entered his mouth.

He gagged, his eyes bulging as the snake pushed deeper down his throat, thick and glistening, cracking his jaw open until it was grotesquely wide, impossibly unhinged. There was a sound like snapping bone and tearing skin. His throat bulged as the snake pushed on and on, its length disappearing further and further.

"Ask me to stop," Clara said, and her grin grew wider.

Caleb's eyes rolled around in his head but his body stayed still as the end of the rattler's tail vanished behind his tongue.

The brothel stayed frozen. Silence lay heavy over the crowd. All eyes were on Clara and Caleb, as she crouched in front of him, as if waiting for something.

His belly bulged then, a slow, grotesque ripple beneath his skin. A single tear swelled in one eye and slipped down his cheek.

"Ask God for forgiveness," Clara hissed, and now her smile nearly split her face in half.

Then, with a sickening crack and a violent explosion of gore, the Diamondback burst from Caleb's middle, ripping through him from the inside out.

Now, finally, they screamed. The crowd scattered, stumbling over furniture, crashing into each other as they fought their way to the door. Glasses and bottles toppled to the floor, glass shattering and chairs flying, bodies thrashing and clawing at each other, desperate for escape. Someone knocked an oil lamp over, and it landed in a pool of spilled whiskey. The floor ignited.

Clara ignored the chaos around her. She rose, slow and steady, her eyes regarding Caleb's corpse with satisfaction.

The snake, now slick with blood and flesh, slithered from his ruined belly and made its way back to its master. Clara bent to meet it, and it wound its way up her arm, across her shoulders, finally settling around her throat like a string of wedding pearls.

The flames rose around them, climbing the drapes and dancing up the walls. Finally, when the smoke curled thick around her, and the flames licked at Caleb's limp body, she turned and walked out into the night.

The black mare was waiting, pawing the earth eagerly, its eyes gleaming with the reflection of the flames.

She climbed into the saddle and flicked the reins.

The wide black night stretched out before her, greeting her with open arms.

She rode west, toward the ranch of the god-fearing man who would have been her husband.

The preacher was dead. The assaulter was ash. And the man who broke his vow? He was next.

The wind caught in her hair as the horse picked up speed, surging forward. Behind her, the brothel burned, and screams followed her into the dark.

The preacher's daughter was gone. What rode out of town that night beneath the pale eye of the watchful moon was something entirely different. Something terrible and divine. Something sinful and glorious. Something vengeful and holy.

Some say Clara Cartwright never made it out of the fire.

Others say that something else walked out of the smoke wearing her skin.

Some say she still rides the night beneath the stars—her black mare cutting swiftly through the dark, her white dress trailing in the wind, serpent bound and wrathful.

Waiting.

For the next man who doesn't listen when a woman says *no*.

For the next man who is bold enough to lay his hands where they don't belong.

And when he does, she'll come.

Not a girl.

Not a ghost.

Just the price you pay for touching what isn't yours.

MIDNIGHT AT DEADWOOD STATION

A DYLAN DECKER STORY

C.M. SAUNDERS

CHAPTER 1

Somewhere between Denver and Salt Lake City, 1883

THE BARREL of the revolver hovering inches away from Dylan's nose not only demanded his attention but filled his entire world. From his seated position it resembled a long, dark tunnel, but with no speck of light at the end. He squirmed as the gaze of the man holding the gun flicked to Dylan's holster and back to his face.

Dylan knew what his aggressor was thinking. He was nervous. Twitchy. He saw the gun on Dylan's right hip, and right now he was debating whether or not to ask Dylan to unholster it and hand it over. To do so carried a huge risk. This man knew next to nothing about Dylan. He might be an expert sharpshooter, and quicker than lightning. Inviting him to draw his gun might be a death warrant. Predictably, the man with the gun thought better of it.

"Put your hands behind your head and lace them fingers nice n' tight," he demanded instead.

In other words, keep your hands well away from that gun, mister.

This guy was no idiot. Unfortunately. Because given just half a chance, Dylan would have shot him in the face. He must be in his forties, maybe late thirties if he'd had an especially hard life, which most people did. Even so, you don't get to be that old without being cautious.

Dylan did what he was told. There was a time and place to make a fuss, and this was neither.

Darkness pressed against the train, obscuring the featureless scenery that had been whooshing past by for the past five hours. The speeding train was snaking its way through mountains and gorges on the vast Denver & Rio Grande Western Railroad, and things had just taken a dramatic turn for the worse.

He knew this gig had been going too smoothly. Escort Mr. Waltham and his good lady wife on their trip, they said. It'll be a piece of cake, they said. After they arrived safely in Salt Lake City he could get on the train right back to Denver, pick up his horse, Skydance, and carry on with his life.

$200 for a three-day job (four if he decided to stop overnight in Salt Lake City) was something he was in no position to turn down. He didn't even question why the couple needed an escort. Until now.

Dylan glanced over at Mr. Waltham sitting opposite him. The frail old man was shrinking back in his seat, trembling fingers splayed before him. It was difficult to tell whether he was pre-emptively surrendering or holding out his hands in a defensive gesture.

Not that it mattered.

His wife Katrina, at least twenty years his junior, sat next to him, her arms held straight up in the air and eyes fixed straight ahead. Anyone would think she'd never been robbed before.

"Where are the emeralds?" the man with the gun said, still pointing his weapon at Dylan but addressing Mr. Waltham.

"I-I'm sure I don't know what..."

"Cut the nonsense!" the would-be robber growled, spittle flying from his mouth. "You are Henry J. Waltham, and you're carrying over a thousand dollars worth of pretty green and blue emeralds."

"H-How..."

"Never mind that. Give. No sudden movements, mind."

Visibly shaking, Waltham reached into a pocket in his tunic and withdrew a small velvet bag, the contents chiming like tiny bells.

"Very good," the robber said, smirking. "Now give me the real bag before I put a hole in your forehead."

Waltham froze. He shot Dylan a glance. He seemed to be imploring Dylan to do something. Get them out of this mess. And true, that was technically what Dylan had been hired for. But what could he do, exactly? One wrong move could see them all killed. No doubt this guy wasn't alone. The guard's uniform he wore suggested he was just one part of a large, well-oiled operation, and he and his buddies probably had a tried-and-tested formula. Right now they were systematically going from carriage to carriage, stripping passengers of their money, valuables, and dignity. $200 wasn't worth getting killed for. And if Waltham disagreed, Dylan would be happy to give him his money back. At least now it was clear why he'd felt the need for an escort in the first place.

"I won't ask you again," the robber urged, growing impatient. "Hand it over."

Grumbling under his breath, Waltham delved into his tunic again and withdrew another bag identical to the last.

"Open it," the gunman demanded.

Sighing, Waltham did has he was told. Just as the robber had intimated, the velvet purse was full of precious stones gleaming under the carriage lights.

"That will do," the gunman said, swiping the purse and stuffing it into his own pocket. Then he glared at Dylan. "What about you, big fella?"

"What about me?" Dylan replied, trying his damnedest to keep his anger under wraps, despite wanting to pick this scrawny little rat up and wring his neck like a Christmas turkey. "I ain't got no bag of emeralds."

"No, but you have at least two hundred dollars on you. Hand it over. Slow, now."

Dylan paused. Watching this bastard rob his client was one thing, but sitting back while he was robbed himself was something else entirely. He ran through his options in his head, while Waltham and his wife watched on imploringly.

Damn it. Even his two hundred dollars wasn't worth three lives. It was just money. It comes and goes. If he lost this, he would just have to make some more. That was the best thing about money. You could always make more.

"Fine," he said, unlacing his fingers.

"Use your left hand, hotshot," the gunman ordered. "And don't forget to take it real slow, like. If I even think you're gonna try summin' I'll shoot you dead and take the money anyway. Makes no odds to me."

Keeping his right hand on his head, Dylan reached into the front pocket of his jeans with the other and pulled out a roll of bank notes.

"Drop it on the floor."

Again, Dylan did as he was told. Then he watched as the gunman stooped to retrieve the money, never taking his gaze, or his gun, off Dylan. If anyone in this carriage was going to try something, now would be the time.

Nobody did. The carriage was two thirds mostly empty, and at this late hour most of the passengers were asleep. The few that were still awake probably didn't even know there was a robbery taking place.

Waltham was probably thinking along the same lines. The old man wasn't armed. Not that Dylan could see, anyway. Men of distinction often didn't carry guns, even when their pockets were full of precious stones. Most of them saw it as uncouth, and hired men like Dylan for such dirty work instead.

"Now, get on your feet," the gunman growled.

"What the devil for?" Dylan protested. "You cleaned us out already."

"Just do it."

Slowly, Dylan rose from his seat. At full height he stood at least four or five inches taller than the robber and was sure he could take him in a fight. But that meant very little with a gun pointed at your face. He knew when he replayed these events in his head later he would be full of regret, wishing he had done this, or done that. He could make himself a hero. Or he could make himself dead. Sometimes you just have to admit defeat and hold your hands up. In this case, literally.

"Move," the robber said.

"Where?"

"That way," the robber said, jabbing his revolver in the direction of the nearest door. Dylan complied, grimacing when he felt the barrel of the gun pressing into the small of his back.

"Where are we going?"

"Just walk."

Dylan did as he was told, stepping into the aisle and moving slowly and deliberately down the narrow aisle separating the two banks of seats.

This couldn't be good. He searched for an escape route, but saw none. He focused instead on walking in a straight line, which was harder than it should have been. The last thing he needed was to lose his balance and make the gunman think he was making a move.

At the end of the aisle was a door leading into the next carriage, and just before it another door to allow passengers on and off the train.

Dear God.

"Open it."

With a sick feeling in his stomach, Dylan again did what the gunman asked. He could see where this situation was headed, and hoped he was wrong. The moment he opened it, the wind ripped the door out of his hand and it slammed forcefully against the side of the train. The sound of the wheels on the tracks was almost deafening.

"Now jump."

"What?" Dylan protested. "You can't be serious."

"I am deadly serious. Jump and take your chances, or stay here and get shot. Choice is yours."

The wind buffeting his hair, Dylan peered into the empty space beyond the open door, hoping to catch sight of some lights that could indicate a settlement or dwelling. How long had it been since the train had last passed through a town of any description? An hour? More? There was nothing but wilderness out there.

"There has to be another way," Dylan protested, all the while knowing he was just delaying the inevitable.

The robber pressed his revolver into Dylan's back, nudging him off the speeding train. He instantly slipped into survival mode. How fast were they going? He knew he had to not just step off but leap, otherwise he risked being dragged under the wheels.

That might be exactly what the robber wanted. Even if Dylan managed to clear the tracks, there was a good chance he would

end up smashed on rocks, anyway. It was so dark, he couldn't see anything. It would save the robber a job.

Taking what might be his final breath, Dylan gritted his teeth and jumped into the darkness.

CHAPTER 2

DYLAN FELT WEIGHTLESS, as if suspended in the air, for what seemed like an eternity. He was profoundly aware of two things; the train thundering on without him, and the ground rushing up to meet him.

And then he collided with it.

He landed on his left side with a bone-crunching thud, hissing loudly as the wind was knocked out of him. He rolled several times, bumping and jarring various parts of his body as he went, until finally his battered body came to a stop as the sound of the train grew distant.

Dylan didn't move for a long time. It was partly fear that kept him on the ground, knowing movement would ruthlessly expose any injuries he may have suffered. In this case, ignorance really was bliss. There was pain, seemingly emanating from a dozen different points, but as long as he stayed still, he could manage it and pretend he was okay. He may even have passed out for a while. Cocooned in darkness, there was no way of knowing.

When he opened his eyes some unknown time later it was still dark, the cold was seeping into his bones, and the silence was thick and foreboding. Something scurried over his face, something with a lot of legs, making him frantically paw at it. Were there scorpions around here? Venomous spiders? Probably.

Slowly, deliberately, he sat up and flexed his limbs one by one. Nothing appeared to be broken, which had been his main concern. Next, he wiggled his head from side to side. There was a little discomfort, but the fact he was able to wiggle his head at all ruled out serious injury. Then he patted himself down looking for wet patches indicative of a puncture. When he found none, he eventually allowed himself the smallest sliver of hope. He might get out of this alive, after all. His sense of optimism was accentuated when the sun chose that moment to peak over the mountains in the distant east, illuminating the landscape with golden rays.

However, the budding flame of hope that had sparked to life was extinguished soon after when there was enough sunlight for Dylan to see where he was. He was in the middle of nowhere.

Wonderful.

The light also allowed him to assess his injuries more accurately. Both knees were grazed and bleeding, his pants ripped and the skin sheared off, there was a lump the size of a hen's egg on his forehead, and a dull throb in his shoulder. His hands were peppered with tiny abrasions, and he knew there were probably hundreds more up and down his battered body. Thankfully, none of his injuries were severe enough to stop him walking, which was just as well because there might be a lot of that in his future.

Wincing as bolts of pain racked his body, Dylan struggled to his feet. Then, he took inventory. Given what he had endured, he considered himself lucky to still be in possession of his Colt and around a dozen spare bullets threaded through his belt. He had also somehow managed to retain the Derringer hidden in his boot. Fat lot of good that did. Still, he should be able to hold his own if he found himself in a gunfight.

The thought made him chuckle to himself. Chance would be a fine thing.

As well as his pistols, Dylan was also in possession of his faithful

Bowie knife, which would probably turn out to be the most valuable tool of all. Finally, he checked his pockets, turning them inside out to make sure he didn't miss anything. Apart from half a box of matches and a length of yarn he didn't even know was there, they were empty. He was reminded of the $200 he had been relieved of on the train and his cheeks flushed with anger and shame, not that any amount of money could help him now.

And that wasn't the worst of it.

He didn't have any supplies. Not a lick of food or water. A man could survive for weeks without food or shelter, even out here in the remote wilderness. But without water he would be dead within days.

With a deepening sense of despair, Dylan took stock of his surroundings. There were mountains on either side, those to the south a lot closer than those to the north, and tangled, lush, vegetation as far as he could see in all directions. There were no buildings, the only man-made construction being the train tracks disappearing into the distance. With no other option Dylan started walking, using the tracks to guide him. At least he knew he would be traveling in a relatively straight line and they had to lead somewhere, even if he had to walk all the way back to Denver.

He didn't push the pace. With no destination in mind, there was no point. Instead, he opted for a steady speed to conserve energy. Even so, within a couple of hours he was battling both exhaustion and a raging thirst. Every step sent shards of pain shooting up his legs and through his body. He had long since taken to walking on the tracks themselves, placing his feet carefully on each timber sleeper, rather than fight his way through the spiky undergrowth which might be concealing any manner of hazard. Discarded traps and bits of machinery left over from the railroad were a possibility, but rattlers were his biggest fear. Getting bitten by one out here would be a death sentence.

With the sun high in the sky, he stopped and dropped to his haunches to rest.

How far had he walked?

It felt like thirty miles, but realistically it was probably more like a quarter of that. He looked down. His clothes were damp with sweat and his pants caked with dried blood from a dozen cuts and gouges, some of which still oozed. He had grown convinced he had cracked a few ribs. It hurt to breathe. And by now his neck was so stiff and sore he could only move his head a fraction in either direction before the pain forced him to move his shoulders too, followed by the entire top half of his body. All things considered, he was about as agile as a scarecrow.

Still, it could have been a lot worse. Luckily for him, the bushes and dense vegetation lining the tracks had broken his fall.

Flexing his toes he realized he was developing blisters to add to his catalogue of injuries. He could feel them popping, filling his socks with puss. He briefly considered taking off his boots for a while, but didn't because if his feet swelled up he might not be able to get them on again and would have to continue this journey to nowhere barefoot.

"What a damn mess," he said, his low voice momentarily carrying on the gentle breeze before being lost in the commotion kicked up by a small group of grouse taking to the air.

On he walked through the hottest part of the day, his pace decreasing seemingly by the step as he pushed through the pain. Once or twice he felt light-headed and swayed on his feet, or took a clumsy misstep that may have sent him crashing to the ground when the world suddenly tilted forty-five degrees. He saw deer and wild hog, and at one point he paused to catch his breath and heard an ominous rustling sound in the undergrowth. He slowly drew his Colt, cocked the hammer, and aimed in the general direction of the noise, ready to shoot anything that posed a threat. He breathed a sigh of relief when a curious skunk poked its head out of the bushes, regarded Dylan with a look of utter distaste, then scurried off back into the undergrowth.

He took a brief foray off the tracks in search of water; a stream or a pond, but was beaten back by the unforgiving terrain. In places it was like trying to fight his way through a jungle, and he resorted to hacking at the offending greenery with his Bowie knife, exhausting himself even more in the process.

A while later he began to develop a dull throb in his middle, which kept getting worse. Always the pessimist, he began to wonder whether he'd done some internal damage. Busted a kidney or something. Besides that, he badly wanted to pee. Or thought he did. But held it in for as long as he could because he didn't want to lose any more fluids. Fluids had been leaving his body one way or another most of the day and pretty soon he was going to be a dried up husk. Someone would stumble across his desiccated corpse six months from now, probably still standing here on these train tracks with his dick in his hand trying to pee.

Don't he stupid, his internal dialogue said, delivering what felt like a solid kick to an already damaged set of ribs. If you died out here the animals would rip you apart and scatter your bones far and wide. Some of them might not even be gracious enough to wait until you were dead. Weak and incapacitated would be good enough. It was only a matter of time before he came across a coyote or a wolf. Or a coyote or a wolf came across him. They would be out on the hunt at dusk, and by then he might represent an easy dinner. He hoped he would still have the strength left to fight them off, not that it required much effort to point a gun and pull a trigger.

He couldn't take it any more. Slowing his limping frame down to a complete halt, he looked around, just in case, unzipped his fly, and reached inside.

Jesus. His nuts had retreated far into his body and his John Thomas was the size of a thimble. He was horrified, and strangely embarrassed, wondering if it would ever be able to recover from this debilitating ordeal. When he finally peed, the liquid was green and streaked with blood.

The last thing Dylan wanted was to spend the night out in the open in an unfamiliar area, but he was exhausted and didn't think he could go much further. He was scanning his surroundings for somewhere to set up camp for the night when something in the distance caught his eye. Was that a building? Off to the side of the railroad tracks?

That could only mean one thing.

A station.

CHAPTER 3

AT FIRST DYLAN thought he was hallucinating, or seeing a mirage. Was Mother Nature mocking him? Or maybe he was just imagining things, a further indication of his slow descent into madness. He squeezed his eyes shut, counted to ten, and opened them again.

The building was still there.

His heart rate quickened, and he set off walking again, now with more purpose and vigor, most of his niggling pain drowned out by adrenaline.

As the building slowly came into focus, Dylan was able to move his aching neck muscles just enough to see that it was a decent-sized, two-story structure. Painted on the side was the word Deadwood. Fitting name for something this far out in the sticks.

Summoning the last of his energy and channelling it towards his legs, Dylan stumbled up the steps leading to the station entrance and burst through the double door.

The waiting room was deserted. But at the far end was a counter manned by a short, wispy little fellow wearing glasses and wearing a little black hat sitting behind a desk below a bold green sign reading TICKETS. In the opposite corner was a tiny kiosk selling snacks, and in another stood an empty coat stand. Benches lined the perimeter of the room and in the middle was a central pillar. As he passed, Dylan noticed a slate plaque mounted on it.

THIS IS TO COMMEMORATE THE LIVES LOST ON TUESDAY, JULY 21, 1873: DEAN WHITLOCK SAVAGE, MORPHEUS OIST, RIPLEY FLYNN, ARCHIE MULDOON, THEODORE STOUT.

The words came together in Dylan's mind long enough to make sense, then melted away into the ether. He had other things to think about. Staggering up to the ticket counter on wounded knees and blistered feet, he croaked, "Give me water."

The station master's gaze drifted over Dylan's disheveled appearance down to the Colt at his side. He seemed to be weighing up how dangerous this interloper was. Seemingly satisfied, he nodded at a blue door semi-hidden behind the coat stand. "There's a tap in the washroom. Been piped in since last summer."

Dylan nodded his thanks, entered the tiny washroom, and went straight to the washbasin clinging to the wall. He turned the handle of the brass tap, and almost sank to his knees with relief when a torrent of lukewarm water rushed forth. It looked clean enough to drink, and he was in no mood to question it.

Cupping his hands, he slaked his thirst, drinking even as it threatened to come back up. Then he splashed some water over his face and neck, washed his hands, and did his best to rinse off some of his wounds. By the time he finished he felt rejuvenated, and marched out of the washroom like a new man.

"You look a lot better for that," the wispy station master manning the counter said. Dylan could now see he wore a name patch reading LLOYD COMBER.

"Yeah, getting thrown off a moving train doesn't do a whole lot for your appearance," Dylan replied with a wry smile. He had no idea what he was going to do now. His plan had never extended to what might happen should he get this far. But he was in no hurry to leave. It would be getting dark soon. "It's pretty quiet up this way, eh? Haven't seen another soul all day."

"Sure is," Comber replied. "Truth be told, it's a little too quiet. Especially if you listen to the suits at the top. This is one of the stations being phased out. Had our marching orders, so to speak. We'll be gone in eight months, and Deadwood station will be left to wrack and ruin like most of the others."

"Ain't that a pity," Dylan said. This, he supposed, was the price of progress. Little pockets of civilization were all too often abandoned in the name of profit.

"'Course it was different back when the slate mine was open and the village was bustling. When the mine closed a few years ago, all those people were left with no jobs and had to move elsewhere. Most migrated south. I'm surprised the station has lasted this long, to be honest with you. I think they plain forgot about us for a while. As long as the pay check keeps coming, we'll keep manning the post. Serve one customer or serve a hundred, I get paid the same."

"Absolutely. How many of you work here?" Dylan asked, curious as to why the station master was using the term 'we' when he appeared to be alone. Maybe it was a company thing. Something drilled into him during training to make the operation seem larger than it was, or to act as a deterrent to would-be robbers.

"Just me, these past couple years," the station master replied, cocking an eyebrow. "I sell the tickets, take inquiries, keep the place clean, even run the snack stall other there when there's a need for it. Would you be wanting any snacks?"

"Not at the moment, thanks," Dylan replied. He was still thinking how he could broach the subject of being penniless. He didn't even have a ticket stub. Katrina Waltham had been responsible for keeping those.

"There used to be a gal working part time in the snack kiosk, but they did away with her position a long time ago. Now, I do everything around here. I live upstairs so it isn't as if I have a long commute. As you can see, it doesn't get very busy. In fact, whole days go by when we don't see a single soul. You could say the writing's been on the wall since Black Tuesday."

"What's Black Tuesday?" asked Dylan, interest piqued.

"Probably the darkest day in the history of the whole county," the station master said, an expression of regret slipping over his face. "Happened ten years ago this very day, funnily enough. Five people died, including a six-year old boy by the name of Theodore Stout."

"That's terrible," Dylan said, suddenly feeling the weight of sorrow that accompanies news of anybody dying so long before their time. "How did it happen?"

"One of the local men who worked the slate mine, Archie Muldoon was his name, built up some serious gambling debts. Nasty piece of work, by all accounts. With work already on the slide, there was no way he could settle his bills so he decided to skip town on the midnight train. The bookie, fella by the name of Morpheus Oist, got wind of his plan and headed up here with an associate to stop him. It was a busy station in them days, even for the midnight train. The waiting room was packed out. Guns were drawn, shots were fired, and Muldoon took young Theodore hostage. He was killed during the shoot-out, along with the bookie, his associate, and a bystander. That tragedy was the last straw for Deadwood. 'Course, the real tragedy is, the whole thing was just a big misunderstanding."

"For real?"

"Yeah, nobody's quite sure of the details," Comber the stationmaster admitted. "They tried to cover it up and brush what had happened under the carpet, so it became this big open secret. Everybody had their theories. But theories mean nothing."

"What do you know about how it all went down?"

"It was pandemonium they say," replied the station master. "A lot of shooting and screaming, and I imagine, a lot of running and hiding. When the shooting finally stopped, five were dead. As I said,

Deadwood was going downhill anyway, but when the only way in and out of the place becomes the scene of a massacre it really hits your popularity."

"I imagine so," Dylan replied. "Speaking of trains, what time will the next one be through?"

"In about two hours."

"That will do," Dylan replied. He had no idea how he was going to pay for the ticket, but he had two hours to think of something.

"Afraid that train is not scheduled to stop here," the station master said.

"Are any trains scheduled to stop here?"

"Of course. The midnight train through to Salt Lake City stops here every time it comes through on this date, even if no passengers get on or off."

"Once a year?"

"Yip."

"What for?"

"As a tribute to those who lost their lives on Black Tuesday. Most of the people here that day were waiting for it. There's a plaque over on the pillar to commemorate it."

"Yeah, I saw that."

"You still look a mess, friend. Why don't you rest on one of them benches over there and I'll wake you up before the train comes?"

"You would do that?"

"Why wouldn't I?"

"Sounds like a plan," Dylan agreed. Right then, nothing sounded better than a nap and the benches were looking very inviting.

CHAPTER 4

DYLAN'S EYES SNAPPED OPEN.

Where was he?

The last thing he remembered was being in some old train station. Deadwood? He was still in the same place. But something was different. No, not something. Everything. There were people everywhere, every seat on every bench taken with others forced to stand in little groups. The low murmur of conversation reverberated around the room.

Suddenly feeling guilty, Dylan swung his legs off the bench in the desperate hope that nobody had seen him stretched out and taking up three seats.

Or tried to.

He'd forgotten about his injuries, but was swiftly and mercilessly reminded.

How long had he been asleep?

It was daylight. Why hadn't the station master woken him up like he said he would?

He rested his elbows on his knees and tried to take in what was happening.

It wasn't just the people.

There was a young woman standing at the snack kiosk, smiling broadly as she handed something to an elderly woman and accepted payment. Didn't the station master say that position had been mothballed? Even the atmosphere had changed. Before it had been stuffy and oppressive. Now, it was buoyant and convivial.

Dylan took a couple of deep breaths and tried to let the steady hum of laughter and conversation calm him. It didn't matter that he preferred his own company to that of other people. This was the situation he found himself in and he had to deal with it. What mystified him most was what had happened between him laying down his head at an almost deserted Deadwood station, and then waking up. Judging by the amount of activity, quite a lot had happened. How could he have slept through it all?

Maybe he was still dreaming.

That must be it.

He thought about pinching himself to make sure, then thought better of it. He had enough injuries. Besides, if this really was a dream, it was turning out a pretty nice one as far as dreams go and he wasn't going to spoil it by trying to wake himself up. No way, brother. He was going to ride this wave to its natural conclusion.

"You okay, mister?"

Dylan turned sharply. Too sharply, the action sending white hot bolts of pain down his side. Sitting next to him was a young boy who couldn't have been more than six or seven years old. "Had better days," he said. "Nothing you or anyone else can do about it now. I'll just put it down to experience, I guess."

"Want some licorice?"

"Huh?"

"Licorice," the boy repeated, holding out a small black chunk he had just unwrapped for himself.

Dylan accepted the offer and munched down hungrily, moaning out loud as the sudden explosion of sweetness kicked his saliva glands into overdrive. "Goddamn kid. That stuff is delicious."

"Yep," the boy replied, as if it were a common fact everybody should know. "Have some more." He pressed another piece of licorice wrapped in grease paper into Dylan's palm.

"Thanks, kid," Dylan said, slipped the candy into his pocket. "Don't mind if I keep it for later, do you?"

"Nope."

"Who are you here with?" Dylan asked, "Are you lost or something?"

"Lost? Of course not. I'm waiting to meet my aunt Shandy off the next train. She's my favorite aunt, though don't tell auntie Beatrice I said that. Or aunt Gert. She's probably more scary than Beatrice. Shandy is the nice one. And she's *really* nice."

"Okay, good to know," Dylan replied.

"Aunt Shandy might bring some peppermint sticks with her. She gets the good stuff up in Denver. If you're still around when she gets here I'll see if I can get one for you if you want."

"The good stuff you say?"

"Oh yeah," the boy agreed. "Gotta be careful cuz there's some lousy peppermint sticks going around. Cheap and nasty." The boy pulled a face, as if being gifted an inferior peppermint stick was the worst thing in the world. And in his world, it probably was.

Where did all that innocence go? Dylan wondered. And how did kids even survive in the real world?

"What's your name, kid?"

"Theodore Stout. Pleased to meet you," the boy switched his bag of licorice to his left hand and held out his right ramrod straight.

"I'm Dylan. Very happy to make your acquaintance, young mister Theodore Stout."

The boy giggled.

Theodore Stout?

Dylan frowned. How did he know that name?

His thoughts were derailed when two men entered the station; the first small in stature but impeccably turned out in a black suit and hat, and his companion a much larger specimen with a rotund belly and a red face. The duo stopped in the doorway.

"We're looking for Archie Muldoon," the smaller man said authoritatively. "Anyone here seen him?"

"I'm here," came a voice from the other side of the waiting room. "What's your business?"

An expectant hush fell over the room and Dylan noticed several nervous-looking bystanders exchanging worried looks. The tension was palpable.

"We have a little problem to iron out," the man in black said. "Word is you owe someone a hefty sum of money."

"I don't owe nobody nothin'".

"That isn't what we've been told. And we're here to collect the debt."

"I'm not giving you anything!" The man on the bench suddenly leapt to his feet, drawing his gun in the process. He wheeled around, Dylan guessed to point the weapon at the two men at the station entrance. It was an extreme reaction, but not an unusual one.

The man wasn't experienced with a revolver. That much was clear by the clumsy way he held it, and the way he squeezed the trigger a little too hard and accidentally opened fire.

Luckily, the barrel was pointing toward the floor, and the bullet thudded into the hard wood.

But the man in black and his fat companion didn't know that. They assumed Muldoon was shooting at them, and reciprocated. Muldoon took a bullet in the thigh, the force knocking him clean off his feet. As he fell, he squeezed the trigger of his revolver, the hot lead projectile striking an old man who had been sitting on one of the benches in the temple. His head was rocked viciously to one side then exploded, showering everyone around him with gore and shards of skull. A grey-haired woman who had been sitting next to him slumped over in a dead faint.

That was when the screaming started. If the shooter's intention had been to cause chaos, he certainly achieved his goal. And in double quick time. Half the people in the waiting room all ran toward the only door at the same time, some falling and being trampled underfoot before they got there. Dylan saw one woman get her bearings so hopelessly out of synch she ran head first into a wall, knocking herself dizzy.

The third shot Muldoon fired appeared to catch the fat man with the red face in the upper chest, the impact spinning him around before he disappeared from view while his companion ducked for cover behind the pillar.

From Dylan's position at the back of the waiting room, he had a clear view of both men. The man in black seemed remarkably unbothered by it all. An oasis of calm in a world of chaos. He held his gun at his side, the hammer cocked, as he scanned the drama unfolding before him.

"You got the wrong man!" Muldoon yelled. He was trying to get to his feet, slipping and sliding in the crimson pools of ichor, a look of desperation painted on his face. He looked like a man who knew his race was almost done.

"You killed Flynn," the man in black growled, who through process of elimination Dylan thought must be Morpheus Oist.

"It was self defense!"

"Doesn't matter what you call it. A man's dead, and you were the one that shot him."

The two men, Muldoon and Oist, began facing each other down from across the room, neither willing to take a backward step. Dylan couldn't help wondering what difference it made who won the shoot-out as whoever survived would likely find themselves up on murder charges by the morning.

The waiting room was half empty now, all those still there seemingly stunned into inaction. Faces crowded around the windows and peaked around the door, all anxious to see what happened next.

Dylan turned to his right to check on the kid.

He was gone.

Looking around the room, Dylan couldn't see him.

Then, Muldoon did something unexpected; with his free hand he made a wild swipe for something or someone. There were gasps, and the gaggle of onlookers shrank back out of his reach. All except one.

Theodore.

Muldoon swept the boy up and cowered behind him, using him like a human shield and pointing his gun in one direction then another as everybody still in the waiting room shrieked and cowered.

"Stay back, the lot of ya!" he yelled.

Recognizing Muldoon was momentarily distracted, Oist raised his gun. But before he could pull the trigger, Muldoon saw the threat and fired first. The bullet ripped into the man in black's throat. It must have severed an artery, because the blood immediately sprayed from the wound in a crimson torrent, cascading down the front of his tunic and drenching the floor around him. He dropped the gun as both hands immediately went to his neck as if he thought he could keep the blood in his body using only his fingers. Of course, it was a useless exercise.

Muldoon had no doubt zeroed-in on Theodore because he thought the boy presented an easy target. And given his size and age, perhaps he did. But Muldoon had failed to think it through. No matter which way he looked, Theodore's slight frame protected only around a third of his assailant's body leaving plenty of room for Dylan to aim at.

When the shooting first started Dylan had kept his distance, content to watch how things played out and not get involved. That was before he'd pieced things together. And since Muldoon had elected to involve his little friend, things had changed. Now, he maneuvered himself behind the waiting room's central pillar and managed to lower his hands so they were out at his sides, just inches from his gun belt.

He didn't want to take the shot. He would have to draw his Colt, aim, and not only hit the target but get away a kill shot, all before Muldoon realized what was happening.

But what choice did he have?

In some dark corner of his being, Dylan knew what would

happen if he stayed quiet and let this situation develop naturally. It was already written in the history books. Or, more accurately, on the pillar in the waiting room. He had to be a disruptor. Change the result. And the best way to do that was with a gun.

His eyes met Theodore's across the waiting room and something passed between them. The boy understood.

Time seemed to slow to a crawl, every sense amplified as Dylan reached for his Colt, closed his fingers around the walnut grip, and began to draw.

Alerted to the movement, Muldoon's head snapped around. For one terrible moment, Dylan didn't know whether he was going to train his weapon on him or Theodore, and he guessed the same thing must be running through the minds of everybody else in the place, and maybe even Muldoon's himself. His judgement perhaps affected by shock or blood loss, in the end he opted to address the threat and aimed at Dylan.

All this indecision played right into Dylan's hands, giving him time to draw his gun, cock the hammer, and sight down the barrel. Everything else; the noise, the tension, the gravity of the situation, all faded away, and the target seemed to expand in size until it was unmissable.

Dylan took the shot.

The Colt jerked in his hand as if it was alive, the retort rebounding off the walls.

There was a pause as a deep hush fell over the room, almost as if everyone present was holding their breath. Dylan took a step to the side, hiding more of his body behind the pillar in case he had to fire again.

There was no need. Muldoon's gun clattered on the floor and he staggered backwards. Blood began to run down his face, and when his wounded leg finally gave out and he keeled over, it was plain to see why. Dylan's bullet had entered just below Muldoon's right eye leaving a small, perfectly round black hole. Upon exiting it had blown the back of his head clean off.

Theodore looked remarkably unmoved by it all. Dylan rushed over, picking his way through the detritus that now littered the floor, knelt in front of him, and grabbed the boy's shoulders. "Are you okay, kid?"

"I'm fine," Theodore replied, wiping his mouth and leaving a black trail of licorice on the back of his hand.

"Must breed you kids tough in these parts," Dylan said, amazed.

Now the drama was over, the hum of conversation began to rise, punctuated by the odd sob and a couple of belated screams.

It was time for Dylan to leave. He didn't want to be around when the dust settled. He hadn't technically done much wrong. In fact, you could argue that was the hero of the hour. But even heroes get targets painted on their backs.

Letting go of Theodore's shoulders, Dylan rose to his feet and turned to make for the door. That was when he lost his footing, his boot slipping on the mess Muldoon had made, and suddenly he was in the air. He knew he was in big trouble when he saw his boots high above his head as he plummeted to the floor.

Then everything went black.

CHAPTER 5

DYLAN OPENED HIS EYES. Or thought he did. It was difficult to know for sure. He still couldn't see, and the amount of pain washing over him was unreal. His neck, his shoulder, his ribs, his head. God, his head. His brain felt like it was expanding and contracting, twisting and contorting. Woozily, he straightened himself up, put his head between his knees, and vomited onto the floor.

Where was he?

There was no sign of any demented, soul-sucking demons, so he assumed he wasn't in hell. Yet.

Where else could he be?

Purgatory?

Or was he back in the waiting room at Deadwood Station?

Were they the same thing?

Night had fallen, and there was no light source.

Wait...

He remembered something. Reaching into his pocket, he pulled out the box of matches he had carried with him all day, and struck one. The flame ignited, the sudden brightness making him recoil. After he got his senses back, he looked around.

He definitely was in the waiting room at Deadwood Station. He recognized the benches circling the huge pillar standing in the middle. But now, the waiting room was completely deserted. Even the ticket counter was closed and the station master gone. By the light of the solitary flame, he could see the entire place was scruffy and run-down, as if it hadn't been in use for years.

Dylan walked over to the pillar, more to test his legs than anything. The plaque he was still there.

But now it was different.

He held the match next to it and read the inscription again.

THIS IS TO COMMEMORATE THE LIVES LOST ON TUESDAY 21 JULY 1873: ARCHIE MULDOON, DEAN WHIT-LOCK SAVAGE, MORPHEUS OIST, AND RIPLEY FLYNN.

Now there were four names listed instead of five. One was missing.

Theodore Stout.

The kid.

He hadn't died that day. So had Dylan been sucked into some kind of vortex or time loop that allowed him to change the course of history? Was such a thing even possible?

Don't be ridiculous, he scolded himself. More likely, he had staggered in here exhausted, dehydrated, and half-concussed, sat on the bench and passed out. The whole thing had been a dream, or a sequence of dreams. The station master, the shoot-out, Theodore Stout. He must have read the inscription on the plaque as he passed and his subconscious mind filled in the blanks.

Ouch!

The match burned down to his fingers. All he needed was a burn to add to his list of ailments.

Dylan dropped the spent match to the floor and stomped on it, then reached into his pocket for the box. He froze. His fingers brushed something else. Something firm but yielding, and unmistakably foreign.

He retrieved the object, struck another match, and held it to the light.

It was a piece of licorice wrapped in grease paper. Dylan started at it, the ramifications of his find beginning to sink in.

Theodore had given it to him.

But Theodore had been part of a dream.

Hadn't he?

Then, he became aware of something. A sound in the distance; a steady, rhythmic chug. At first, he thought it must be his imagination. Wishful thinking. But it was getting louder.

There was a train coming.

Everything else temporarily forgotten, Dylan rushed outside the waiting room and looked down the tracks, straining his eyes to see in the darkness. In the distance, he could just make out the blinking lights of a speeding locomotive.

Standing on the station platform, he watched the train get closer and closer, all the while wondering how he could attract the attention of the driver. A match probably wouldn't cut it.

But as the train approached Deadwood Station there was the squeal of brakes and it steadily decreased its speed until coming to a full stop.

Nobody got off.

Alone on the platform, Dylan was reminded of something the station master had said.

"The midnight train through to Salt Lake City stops here every time it comes through, even if no passengers get on or off, as a tribute to those who lost their lives on Black Tuesday."

Apart from the odd flickering oil lamp most of the carriages were in darkness, many of the passengers probably taking the opportunity to sleep, and there was no sign of any guards or other rail workers.

Moving as quickly and quietly as his injuries permitted, Dylan

was able to discreetly open one of the doors and climb aboard, hopefully unseen, just as the train began to pull off again. He watched
through the window as Deadwood station disappeared behind him,
happy to finally be getting away from the place.

CHAPTER 6

DEAR MR WALTHAM,

I trust this letter finds you well. There are several reasons why I felt compelled to write to you. Firstly, I want to inform you of my comparative good health. I don't know if that is something you have consideration for. You could be forgiven for assuming the worst when I was thrown off that train. Secondly, I would like to thank you for the opportunity to work with you, and apologize for not fulfilling my duties. As you saw for yourself, it would be unfair to lay the entirety of the blame for that unfortunate sequence of events upon my shoulders, which brings me to my main point.

For the true perpetrator of the crimes you witnessed, including the theft of your impressive collection of jewels, look no further than your good lady wife, Katrina. I understand your first notion might be to leap to her defense, but I implore you to do me the courtesy of explaining myself. The man who robbed us was most certainly in possession of some privileged information. He knew you would be carrying two bags of emeralds, one a decoy, and he knew I was in possession of $200 in cash.

How could he have known these things? I certainly didn't tell him. I didn't know about the decoy bag. Heck, you didn't even tell me you were carrying emeralds. And maybe if you had, I would have been a whole lot more vigilant. Anyway, the only person close enough to you to know these things is Katrina. As to why she would have you robbed well, it's not my place to speculate, but it crossed my mind that she might be romantically involved with the man who robbed you and pushed me off the train. Then again, she might just have wanted to get her hands on those emeralds in which case your life may still be in danger. I stopped trying to map the mind of a woman long ago. That way lies madness.

One last thing, Mr. Waltham. On the railroad tracks somewhere between Denver and Salt Lake City is a station called Deadwood. I would give it a wide berth if I were you.

Yours,
DD

HORROR
ON THE
RANGE

ED DOWNES

Ed Downes writes stories that are suspenseful, sometimes scary, and always thrilling, where things are not always what they seem. His entertaining yet vulnerable characters usually find themselves thrust into situations that appear to be no win. Ed is the author of many short thriller fiction stories including Qalupalik, Regrets, and Dr. Bonz.

He is currently putting the finishing touches on his first novel Frozen Echoes and he has recently completed his Master of Fine Arts degree in Writing Popular Fiction from Seton Hill University. A publishing industry marketing strategist by day, and novelist by night, he is a Boston native, and a lover of tennis, skiing, and scuba diving.

He currently lives in Raleigh, NC, most likely reading or writing thriller fiction or doing fun stuff with his wife Jeanie and two daughters Melissa and Jessica.

eddownes.com

 instagram.com/eddowneswrites

 facebook.com/eddownes

 x.com/eddownes

MADI HAAB

Madi Haab (she/her) is a queer and neurodivergent writer of Moroccan descent from Tiohtià:ke/Montréal. She draws inspiration from her mixed cultural heritage and identities to explore the liminal and interstitial through speculative fiction and poetry. Her work has appeared in Augur Magazine, Haven Speculative, carte blanche magazine, and more. When not writing, she dabbles in art and singing, and likes video games and afternoon naps a little too much.

www.madihaab.com

 bsky.app/profile/madihaab.com

DESIREE HORTON

Desiree Horton is a horror author and enthusiast living in the heart of Washington. You can find her sitting outside, playing with her dogs, or adventuring with her husband and two children. Her full-length works, Midnight Mother, Of Teeth and Pine, What Comes From Between, and Tell Me How it Ends, can all be found on Amazon or your local bookstore. Find her short stories peppered into numerous anthologies, or on scraps of paper she accidentally throws away.

authordesireehorton.my.canva.site

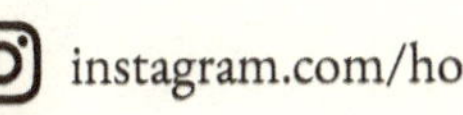 instagram.com/horrortonwritesabook

facebook.com/desiree.horton.31

RICHARD LAU

Richard Lau is an award-winning writer who is published in magazines, newspapers, and anthologies, as well as in the high-tech industry and online.

SCOTTY MILDER

Scotty Milder is a writer, filmmaker, and educator living in New Mexico. He received his MFA in Screenwriting from Boston University, and his award-winning short films have screened at festivals all over the world. His independent feature film "Dead Billy" is available to stream.

He has sold more than 50 short stories, and his fiction has appeared in Dark Matter Magazine, Cosmic Horror Monthly, anthologies from Dark Moon Books, Dark Peninsula Press, Undertaker Books, Sentinel Creatives, and others.

He teaches film production at Santa Fe Community College and the University of New Mexico.

www.scottymilder.com

instagram.com/scottymilderhorror
facebook.com/scottymilderwrites
threads.com/@scottymilderhorror

E.M. OTERO

EM Otero is a Puerto Rican author and lover of all things weird. When he isn't writing, he is busy being a husband and father. While working outside or hiking, he loves to take pictures of plants, insects, and anything else he finds interesting or strange. He loves showing his daughter and wife the curious things in nature.

His writing is inspired by our weird world, robot anime, horror stories, and science.

www.emoteroauthor.com

instagram.com/e.m._otero

facebook.com/TheHowlingBetweenWorlds

patreon.com/EmOtero

MICHAEL PICCO

Michael Picco lives in the Colorado high country with a menagerie of monsters — real and imagined. His work has appeared in dozens of anthologies, and he has produced two, award-winning collections: *Scenes From The Carnival Lounge* and *Corpse Honey* (and is working on a third titled: *Tangled In The Shadows*). He is a member of the Denver Horror Collective, The Rocky Mountain Fiction Writers, and the Western Colorado Writers' Forum.

www.michaelpicco.com

instagram.com/Piccoman
amazon.com/author/michaelpicco

C.M. SAUNDERS

Chris Saunders (he/him), who writes fiction as C.M. Saunders, is a writer and editor from South Wales. He has worked extensively in the publishing industry, holding desk jobs ranging from staff writer to associate editor, and is currently employed at a trade magazine. His fiction has appeared in numerous magazines, ezines, and anthologies worldwide, including the Literary Hatchet, Crimson Streets, 34 Orchard, Phantasmagoria, and DOA volumes I and III, while his books have been both traditionally and independently published. He has released six volumes of short fiction and several novellas, the latest being Tethered on 13 Days Publishing. Blood Lake is the second Dylan Decker book, following Silent Mine.

cmsaunders.wordpress.com

facebook.com/CMSaunders01

goodreads.com/horrorjunkie

DEBORAH TAPPER

Deborah Tapper has been published in anthologies, magazines and online. An occasional stargazer, she collects dictionaries and is fascinated by folklore and everything prehistoric. She lives in the middle of nowhere with her understanding partner, drinks too much strong tea and writes at an old desk surrounded by five hundred pet bugs.

J.R. TAYLOR

J.R. Taylor is a horror writer based in Toronto, Canada. She writes creepy fiction, often with themes of feminine rage and "good for her" energy. When she's not writing, you'll find her acting on-screen or in voiceover, bingeing true crime podcasts, watching scary movies, reading an absurd number of books, traveling the world, or hanging out with her cat Nox and dog Daisy.

jtwritesstories.wordpress.com

instagram.com/jt.readsandwrites

tiktok.com/@jt.readsandwrites

PATRICIA THORPE

Patricia Thorpe is a New England-based writer whose work blends psychological depth with atmospheric horror. Her fiction has earned recognition from the Claymore Awards and the Al Blanchard Awards, and her debut horror novel, *Season of the Sixth*, explores the eerie undercurrents of coastal life. When she's not writing, she enjoys cooking, reading, and walking through the woods near her home in north central Massachusetts.

www.pattythorpe.com

D.L. WINCHESTER

D.L. Winchester lives in the foothills of southern Appalachia. A former mortician, his work searches the darkness to find tales worth telling. He is the author of over three hundred obituaries, numerous short stories, and the upcoming Flash Fiction Collection "A Terrible Place." In his spare time, he can be found searching for inspiration in the world around him and trying to keep his children from becoming the next generation of horror villains.

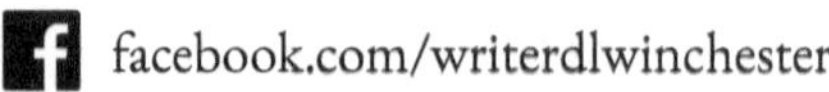 facebook.com/writerdlwinchester

CHLOE YORK

Chloe York, an award-winning abstract painter, insect taxidermist, and owner of a small oddities company, resides in Birmingham, Alabama with her sculptor husband and ferocious daughter in their shared home and studio. When she's not painting seascapes or framing bugs, she can be found in her lair writing fantasy and horror novels.

www.chloe-york.com

 instagram.com/chloe.york.art
 facebook.com/chloe.york.art
 bsky.app/profile/chloe-york.bsky.social

MORE ANTHOLOGIES BY UNDERTAKER BOOKS

Stories to Take to Your Grave: Mortuary Edition

Stories to Take to Your Grave: Wandering Souls

Winter Horrorland

Judicial Homocide

Carnival of Horrors

<u>COMING SOON</u>

Stories to Take to Your Grave: High Seas